Other books by Donald J. Richardson

Dust in the Wind, 2001

Rails to Light, 2005

Song of Fools, 2006

Words of Truth, 2007

The Meditation of My Heart, 2008

The Days of Darkness, 2009

The Dying of the Light, 2010

BETWEEN THE DARKNESS AND THE LIGHT

Donald J. Richardson

authorHOUSE®

AuthorHouse™
1663 Liberty Drive
Bloomington, IN 47403
www.authorhouse.com
Phone: 1-800-839-8640

First published by AuthorHouse   12/7/2010

ISBN: 978-1-4520-9990-3 (sc)
ISBN: 978-1-4520-9992-7 (e)
ISBN: 978-1-4520-9991-0 (dj)

Library of Congress Control Number: 2010917379
Printed in the United States of America

For all my fellow Senior Citizens

Numbers 6:24-26.

Table of Contents

Chapter One

I never set out to serve God. In fact, I'm not sure I even know what serving God means. It's not as if I'm a waitress in a restaurant and God comes in asking for the special. Suppose there is no special? All I ever wanted to do was grow up and become a woman. I don't think that was unreasonable. But whoever my mother was didn't think far enough ahead to allow this to happen for me. The sisters said I was left on their doorstep April 26th, 1921. So that means I'm eighty-nine years old now. How did I get from being an infant left on the Sisters of Mercy Orphanage to being eighty-nine years old? I suppose it is a long, meandering story, but here goes.

The sisters said there was no message left with me, only a name; I was wrapped up in a blanket and placed in a basket. Since it appeared I was a few days old, they agreed that I had been born on April 23rd. This, I found out later, was important as it was also the date usually cited as the birth of William Shakespeare, the playwright. Right from the beginning then, I had a connection whether I knew it or not. Three hundred and fifty-seven years after Shakespeare was born, I was born. Of course, I had no notion of this until years later when I learned the supposed birth date of Shakespeare.

I was an easy baby to care for, they told me. Since the orphanage took in all ages, I seemed to have numerous sisters, all of whom looked after me. Because it was a charitable institution, the Sisters of Mercy Orphanage couldn't provide the residents with many worldly possessions. I don't remember ever having a new dress or new shoes while I lived there. Always we were happy to receive the donated items that parents of children who had grown out of left us.

The sisters discouraged us from claiming specific items of clothing. If a garment became favored by someone, she wasn't allowed to keep it. She was supposed to take something from the clothing storage unit that would fit her and be happy about it. Rarely were we happy, however. There were certain dresses or blouses or sweaters that it seemed all of the girls coveted. Once the sisters discovered this, they made certain that the item was rotated among the girls. If we became too possessive or contentious, they might retire the garment entirely so that no one got it. Their argument was that we should not put too much stock in worldly possessions.

Today, having lived all of those years, I recognize the truth of what the sisters were trying to teach us. Even my books—much as I love them and as few of them as there are—are worldly possessions. I read in *Walden* by Henry David Thoreau that our possessions own us. When I first saw that, I didn't understand. How can a physical object own a person? But after I read on and thought about it, I began to see what Thoreau was getting at and what the sisters had been trying to teach us. Putting too much stock into things is antithetical to what the Bible says; after all, Jesus said, "Sell all your possessions and follow me."

Still, it was hard to resist the urge to want things, especially at Christmas. Each of us was given an orange and a few pieces of hard candy at Christmas. Just having these was satisfying, but if one didn't want to lose the orange, it had to be protected. There were girls who might take it if we didn't watch them. And if we ate the orange, then we would no longer have it.

It was long after I left the orphanage that I realized the exchange of gifts was common among people not brought up by the Sisters of Mercy at their orphanage. For we never received gifts, nor were we encouraged to exchange them. That would have been too worldly, they would have said. Today, this practice is followed by nearly everyone, but then the Sisters of Mercy Orphanage no longer exists. In fact, there may no longer be any orphanages, either. At the time we didn't know, truly, what we were missing, and none of us felt deprived. But children today would feel sorely used if they didn't receive gifts at Christmas. Did this non-giving of Christmas gifts deprive us, or did it prepare us for a more exalted existence? I don't have that worked out yet.

I remember the first time I bought a dress which no one else had worn before me; I was awed. Here was a brand-new dress which no one else had ever worn and which now belonged to me. That happened years later, naturally.

Since I've become a woman on my own I have come to value clothing, perhaps sinfully. Even underclothing seems special to me. At the orphanage we were forced to wear unappealing garments meant to hide our bodies and be seen only by anyone who did the washing. None of us had the least suspicion that undergarments were anything but functional.

Still, life at the orphanage was not oppressive or exacting. Oh, certainly, the sisters expected us to behave properly, to say our prayers and always show courtesy to others, but there was occasional laughter, and we were permitted to cultivate friendships. In fact, as I look back I realize that life there might have been a true definition of a democracy. We were all forced to regard each other as equal, and we were made to behave equally. No one was permitted to lord it over anyone else, even those girls who were naturally prettier than the rest of us. Mary Kay Wilkins, for example, had beautiful blonde hair which just seemed to curl all by itself. Her complexion also was beautiful. But she was treated the same as any of the rest of us, despite her natural beauty. Even in class, the sisters reminded us that those of us who seemed to know most of the answers or who got the highest scores on tests were not permitted to look down on the others. We were imbued with the notion that we were decidedly equal, despite our varying abilities which were not to be overly exalted. Humility was a characteristic of Jesus Christ, and we were expected to emulate Him.

All of us at the Sisters of Mercy Orphanage were assigned duties. When I was just a girl of six, I had to help with gathering dirty dishes and carrying them into the kitchen after meals, gathering dirty clothing to take to the laundry, and sweeping the floors and dusting as needed. But I don't think any of us resented it because we all had out duties. Everyone helped out and no one received special treatment.

At night we slept in a dormitory which was filled with beds. The beds were close enough that we could whisper to each other after lights out, but they were far enough apart that each of us inhabited her own private world. The girls who developed special friendships managed to get beds adjoining and sometimes they even slept together. This wasn't actually permitted as each of us was supposed to sleep alone. But it went on, despite the sisters' disapproval. In fact, they probably knew what was happening, but perhaps seeing no harm in it allowed it to continue.

As I look back, I don't believe there was any harm in it. Someone who felt sad for whatever reason, might be comforted in the arms of a friend, and this sort of comfort we didn't receive any other way. I don't believe that such experiences caused any of the girls to become lesbians or to prefer women over men; they were simply lonely and needed comfort. Without the love of a mother or a father, or even a brother or sister, we were cut adrift, and it was natural, I believe, that we felt isolated and alone at times. Those were the times when we were most vulnerable. Who among us would resist comforting a child who had fallen and skinned a knee? And by the same token who would withhold affection from another person who needed comforting?

School was regimented as was most of our life at the Sisters of Mercy. We had three classrooms—one for the first, second, and third grades; one for fourth, fifth, and sixth; and one for seventh and eighth grades. I do not remember much of my life in the early grades. It has been so long ago and I have seen and experienced so much since then that looking back and trying to remember seems a bit self-indulgent. Even if I could remember, what benefit would it provide?

The sisters worked to try to make school rewarding for us. They observed the holidays and allowed us to pursue our creative interests in making posters or drawing pictures which celebrated George Washington's birthday or Arbor Day or Independence Day. When I was a girl, each of these holidays was regarded as special, and all of us looked forward to them eagerly. The treats we were given were not food or candy as is done today; instead, we were given privileges of drawing or painting or even reading. I seem to remember that both the intermediate grade teacher and the upper grade teacher read to us after lunch every day. Many times the books were chosen with the holidays in mind, so we looked forward to these special days with even more anticipation. And when that holiday was over, we didn't look backward in regret but focused on the next one, looking forward to it. In fact, much of my grade school life I remember as being forward looking, anticipating what was coming next.

Christmas and Easter were very special for us as we celebrated the birth of the baby Jesus and the resurrection of Christ. We also were given a few days vacation from school at Christmas, so that was an additional reason to look forward to the holiday.

Easter, on the other hand, was decidedly more religious. Those who hadn't yet made their first communion were urged to do it on Easter Sunday. This way the experience was made special and easy to remember, although few of us had trouble remembering our first communion. It was simply held in too high esteem by the sisters for us ever to forget it.

Soon after I mastered the alphabet and learned to read, I discovered books on my own. Prior to that I had enjoyed picture books, but now when I found I could actually read for myself, the world opened up into unending potential. I saw that the stories that went along with the pictures enriched the experience, and I began to read with abandon. I don't remember what year it was, but one of the first chapter books I read was *Smoky the Cowhorse* by Will James, an authentic cowboy. I think I must have been nearly ten years old at the time because I already knew something about writing and good grammar. Thus, I was nonplussed by James's apparently ignorant approach to writing. He wrote the way cowboys talked, not the way people wrote in books and, at first, I was somewhat annoyed. Ignoring subject verb agreement and other bugbears of the language, he just seemed to put words down on paper as they came to him. But I was captivated by his drawings of Smoky and of the western life. Maybe these drawings served to redeem his writing for me. Perhaps I saw that grammar wasn't all it was made out to be. All I know is that I loved that book, and once I finished it I re-read it. In fact, I don't recall how many times I did read it.

Then I discovered that James had written other books, and so I read those. I think my favorite after *Smoky* was *Lone Cowboy*, his autobiography. It was exciting to read about his being born on the plains, of living with his friend Beaupre, and heartbreaking when Beaupre was evidently carried away and drowned by a raging stream. Later on I enjoyed his stories of working in the movies in Hollywood.

As a result of reading the Will James books, I determined that I wanted to be a cowboy myself. Since we were already living in San Diego, I could hardly go farther west; in fact, I saw I would have to go east somewhat and north, to Montana or Colorado. The independence of being a cowboy called to me just as strongly as the sirens beckoned Odysseus. But, of course, I couldn't be a cowboy or even a cowgirl. Such dreams were meant to help me transcend my everyday existence, I suppose, to allow me to look past where I was and to dream of a future when I could control my life and not be answerable to anyone else. Such as this are our daydreams made up of.

After I had read Will James, I went on years later to the Eleanor Estes stories of the Moffat family. I suppose it was natural that I identify with Jane, the middle Moffat. Rufus was a boy, and Sylvie was too old for me to identify with. I think I was envious of the family relationship they enjoyed. I endured their poverty during and after World War I, and I enjoyed their triumphs with them on New Dollar Street. I was especially envious that they had a family, even though there was no father.

But by the time I had read about the Moffat family, I was getting too old for such stories. So I set out on a program to educate myself by reading. Naïve as I was, I thought that just reading a book like *The Scarlet Letter* would lead me to become smarter. In fact, it took me years to realize that the mere reading of a book and checking it off from a list didn't foster insight or wisdom; it meant only that I could read. It was only later when I found someone to discuss a book that I could begin to see its true importance. Not only that, I began to see that not all books were worth reading. At first I had the dogged opinion that if I started reading a book I was supposed to finish it. As a result, I waded through *The Brothers Karamazov* without enjoying it one little bit. It was a curse and a trial to try to keep the characters separate, and reading about their involved machinations within the family and their social group was simply not pleasurable. But at the time I think I regarded reading as something like castor oil: to be endured for its own good. If I got some pleasure from it, that was an added benefit, but if there was no pleasure, well I had to finish the book anyway. I wasn't to start anything which I didn't finish. This was a bone-headed attitude it took me years to get past. And I don't remember what book it was that I thought as I was reading, "This is not a good book. I do not have to finish it." Whatever book it was, the thought was a true revelation, akin to seeing a person's soul or character instead of her face, recognizing the actual essence of the person. But once I realized that, I saw that some books were just not intended for me. Some books might come highly recommended, but if they didn't speak to me, I didn't have to listen to them. Their voices were meant for other people's ears or eyes.

I suppose as a result of my reading I did become educated to an extent. Although I didn't fully understand Shakespeare, I read all of his plays, even *Titus Andronicus* and all of the history plays. I can't say I enjoyed all of them, but since it was Shakespeare and I was resolved to become educated, and since educated people knew Shakespeare, then I would read the plays. Probably seeing the plays on stage would have helped immensely. This I suspect from seeing a production of *Romeo and Juliet*. I recognized that it had been edited to leave out some of the nurse's speeches. At times she is quite direct in talking to Juliet. This I suppose might not be appropriate for everyone, but even after being edited it was still Shakespeare, and I enjoyed it. After that I wished I lived in London and could attend the Globe Theatre to see all of the Shakespeare plays.

I have continued to read all of my life, not consistently to educate myself as that, I suppose, was a somewhat misguided notion, but to inform myself and to derive pleasure. After I left the orphanage, I saw I could take control of my life, actually attending motion pictures which we had never seen at the orphanage, of course, and living my own life. I was defining my own rules, fabricating the cloth of my personality as I determined what was or was not moral behavior. When I began earning money, I saw that I no longer had to check books out from the library; I could actually buy and own books myself. This has led to a lifetime habit of purchasing books and holding onto them, even long after I felt any urge to re-read them. Oh, I justified myself, naturally. Instead of smoking or drinking or running around, I read, and books were not anti-social—unless one considered that reading itself is somewhat anti-social.

Today at eighty-nine reading is as important to me as any other activity. I still pray and attend church, but when it comes to what I really love to do when I have a spare moment, and there are more of these as I grow older, I find I prefer to read. I subscribe to some magazines which I read every month, but my favorite reading is history, biography, autobiography, and some fiction. When I was younger, I dived into fiction as a sunburned youngster would dive into a refreshing swimming pool on a June day, but as I have grown older, I find that fiction is less and less satisfying. Of course, there are some books that still attract me, but few works of fiction compare to the actual history of our country or the lives of people like Dolley Madison or George Washington. These people lived, and their lives are instructive to me in a way that fiction rarely achieves. I also like to read the histories of the times I grew up in: the twenties, the thirties, the forties, and some of World War II. I'm not an enthusiast of war stories, but even so when they are told by men who were there, and occasionally women, I love the experience.

When I read *Yankee from Olympus* about Oliver Wendell Holmes, Jr. I was impressed by Holmes' behavior after he retired from the Supreme Court. He was in his early 90s, I believe, but he continued to study and read until he died at age 94. Even then he had a list of books he still wanted to read. This is what I aspire to.

Chapter Two

I don't remember when I first knew about Aimee Semple McPherson. I do recall listening to KFSG radio which Aimee named for Foursquare Gospel-owned. When I first heard her, it was a revelation. A radio was tuned to KFSG, and suddenly a woman was talking. But this was talk the likes of which I had never heard before. This was talk of revelation and salvation. A current of awareness went through me as if I had touched a bare electric wire—something that charged me and my soul, thrilling me.

She spoke of matters I could understand and she used words I knew. She told of a rose which she described—evidently she was holding a rose.

"This rose grew and matured and blossomed with God's help. This beautiful rose symbolizes your soul. If you feed it and water it with prayer and devotion, it, too, will blossom and become beautiful in God's sight. For every soul wants to be like this rose. Every soul wants to become beautiful in God's sight. And it is up to you to let it happen—God wants all of our souls to be beautiful, and what feeling of ecstasy it is to be one of God's blossoms. There is no other feeling like it. All of our souls need this. For this is a way of preparing for God's kingdom after we go on. After we have lived this life, we move on to be with God forever. But in order to be ready, we must prepare. We have to nurture our souls."

This was not a sermon the likes of which we heard Father O'Malley deliver on Sunday morning in the chapel. When Father O'Malley talked, it was in a tone which was easy to listen to but also easy not to concentrate on. I had often daydreamed to Father O'Malley's sermons, so I liked them. Maybe that is the wrong reason to like a sermon, but I did, nevertheless. At times, I closed my eyes and entered a state which seemed to be nearly unconscious. Not that I was unconscious—I was still aware of where I was and what was happening around me—but I seemed to exist apart from my body. This was a pleasant sensation which at times even approached sleep. This was similar to the state one enters just before sleep overtakes a person, or sometimes the half-awake, half-asleep state experienced just before getting up in the morning.

Listening to Sister Aimee was much different from listening to Father O'Malley. I found that I actually wanted to listen to Sister Aimee. She had something to say, and she said it well. Her voice was musical, and it seemed to come right from heaven. How could anybody resist her appeal, I wondered.

After that first time I tried to listen to Sister Aimee whenever I could. I was still at the Sisters of Mercy Orphanage, so I must have been twelve or thirteen at the time. After I had listened to her several times, I began to wonder if I would ever get to see her in person.

There was an extensive article in the newspaper which told all about her mission and the Angelus Temple in the Echo Park area of Los Angeles. The article said the temple, which could seat 5,300 people, was dedicated January 1, 1923, and was filled to capacity three times each day, seven days a week, with Sister Aimee preaching every service. Sometimes the services were very dramatic with all sorts of staging effects and special props. Of course, we couldn't see these on the radio, but I imagined them and wanted to see them for myself.

She and her mother had toured the United States in her "Gospel Car," a 1912 Packard touring car; this was in 1916. After they drove cross country to Los Angeles, she built Angelus Temple and had it paid for within a short time.

The four main beliefs of the Foursquare Gospel were Christ's ability to transform individuals' lives through salvation; holy baptism; divine healing; and gospel-oriented heed to the second coming of Christ. I'm pretty certain I didn't understand all of these when I read them. Not only that, but these beliefs contrasted sharply with those of the Roman Catholic church, so the sisters forbade us to listen to her radio broadcasts. I just couldn't help myself, however. Something in her voice and her message seemed to call to me, to say, "This is the way." My one wish became to get to see Sister Aimee in person and maybe even become like her.

I did finally get to witness one of the services in the Angelus Temple which was inspirational but in a way it was disappointing. By the time I got to Los Angeles, Sister Aimee had had several negative experiences reported on by the newspapers. The most sensational focused on her disappearance from Venice Beach in May, 1926. When she was reported missing, every newspaper ran headline stories about her. I read about this later, of course, as I wasn't old enough to pay attention when it happened.

People had just about given up on Sister Aimee when on June 23rd, she walked in out of the desert in Mexico, saying she had been kidnapped and held for ransom. Many people didn't believe her and eventually she was charged by a grand jury with obstruction of justice. Finally Los Angeles district attorney Asa Keyes dropped all charges on January 27, 1927.

By the time I got to see Sister Aimee she had been married three times. Born Aimee Elizabeth Kennedy in 1890, she married Robert Semple, an evangelist, in 1908. They left for Hong Kong, but he died there of malaria in August, 1910. A month later, Aimee gave birth to a daughter, Roberta.

She married Harold McPherson, an accountant, in 1912, and they had a son, Rolf. However, McPherson didn't like her religious traveling, and they were divorced in 1921. Sister Aimee's final marriage was to David Hutton in 1931, but they were divorced in March, 1934. Most people referred to her as Aimee Semple McPherson, but her real name, including all of her husbands, was Aimee Elizabeth Kennedy Semple McPherson Hutton. I think most of her supporters referred to her simply as Sister Aimee.

The night I got to see Sister Aimee was one of those bright, Los Angeles evenings when everything seemed to be lighted up by God's presence. The light was almost spectral, suggesting an otherworldliness to everything, as if the universe was aware of something special about to happen.

The temple itself was huge, but it was almost filled when I managed to find a seat. The altar or stage was down in front of the tiered seats, and it was raised to permit everyone to see it easily. Behind the altar were the singers in the choir, nearly one hundred of them dressed in beautiful sky-blue robes, spaced evenly around the altar in a half circle so that they appeared to surround the altar itself.

People were talking but not very loudly as we waited for the service to begin. Outside I had noticed several handicapped people, people on crutches or in wheelchairs, slowly and in some cases painfully making their way into the temple. They were here, I supposed, to be healed. Sister Aimee had a reputation for placing her hands on people and actually healing physical defects: causing the blind to see and the deaf to hear. The Sisters of Mercy had ridiculed such claims, but they continued to appear in the newspaper stories, so I wondered if they weren't actually true.

After a short wait while there was music to be heard from the altar, some men entered carrying a shoulder-high platform on which someone reclined. The men were bare to the waist and their upper bodies gleamed as if they had been covered with oil. All of them wore turbans and blowsy, colorful silken pants. At first I couldn't see who was on the platform, but then I realized it was Sister Aimee.

When they got to the altar, the men deposited Sister Aimee who stood and faced the congregation. She was dressed entirely in white which was her customary dress. I know she talked to all of us in the congregation, but when I try to re-create her words or her message, they escape me. Maybe I was under the spell of her magic; maybe I was just so taken by Sister Aimee that all I could do was look and marvel.

I remember that she was in complete charge of the service. Whenever she signaled she was done speaking, the choir sang. I think this was the largest choir I had ever heard, and of course I thought they were beautiful. After a hymn, Sister Aimee would resume her message, addressing everyone in the audience as though we were her personal friends. As I listened, I felt that if only I had a chance to get to know Sister Aimee, she and I could form a bond that would go beyond any other, that we could become sisters in Christ, almost. My heart ached with longing and desire for this connection, but even before the service ended, I realized it could never be. Our lives and worlds were too far apart, and she must have had dozens of friends who had much closer connections to her than I ever could. I also saw that at my age, I would be like a daughter to her—in fact, I was eleven years younger than her own daughter, Roberta.

After the service was ended, a call was made for the sick and the lame to approach the altar. Some had to be carried while others were pushed in wheelchairs. Others were led or helped along by family members or attendants. I had made my way down closer to the front so I could see what was happening.

Sister Aimee approached each of the petitioners carefully and gracefully. At times I could see the perspiration on her forehead, and I began to suspect that this was very exacting work she was doing. I couldn't overhear anything she said because she spoke softly to each person, as if she was a priest hearing a confession. Once this part was over, she laid her hands onto the person, it appeared onto the afflicted area, and entered what looked like a trance. Apparently she was praying or directing all of her power or the power of heaven toward the person under her hands.

Whether anyone believes me or not, I saw people healed that night. Enough has been written about Sister Aimee, in the newspapers, in articles, and in books, that there are actual testimonials from people who were cured. These people were not faking; they were actually healed. How she did it I do not know, and I don't know that anyone else does. Yet she did it. And she did it night after night. I saw crutches thrown away, wheelchairs deserted, hearing aids discarded, and thick glasses removed because they were no longer needed.

I have often wondered what it would be like to witness a true miracle, such as those described in the Bible. How could those few loaves and fishes actually feed thousands of people? How could water be changed into wine? I thought that it would be such a blessing to actually witness such a miracle that a person's life direction would be changed. She could go on with a renewed sense of purpose which would allow her to serve without asking mundane questions about reason or existence. I have found myself wishing for such a miracle at times in my life.

But I did witness Aimee's laying on of hands, and if the people I saw were any evidence, I saw miracles. There are still those who scoff, who say she must have planted people in the audience, but I do not believe that. Nor do I know how she caused it to happen. All I know is that I saw people healed, and their names are available in some of the newspaper articles and some of the books. Those people were healed and they stayed healed. How can this be? I do not know, but I do believe.

I don't recall how long Sister Aimee ministered to the afflicted, but as the evening wore on she eventually had to stop. Even from where I was sitting, I could see she was exhausted. What did it require of her to do this—God's work? What life energy did it suck from her body to lay her hands on these people and serve as a conduit for God's grace? For that's what she was doing. She was actually connecting these people to God. Perhaps it was like electricity. I've been shocked by electricity, and I know how jittery being shocked made me feel. What must it have required of her to carry on this God's work for hours at a time?

Finally, she had to stop. Not everyone had had a chance to have her touch them, but it was late, and there were more services tomorrow. After she blessed everyone and left the alter, the people also left the temple.

Outside, the Los Angeles night was dark and mysterious after the temple experience. I was reluctant to resume my life as I knew I had witnessed something rare and unusual, even miraculous. I didn't pretend to understand then, and I don't understand it today either, so many years later. But I was there. I saw it, and I believe.

Chapter Three

Alexandria is a different and even difficult name. When I was left on the steps of the Sisters of Mercy Orphanage, the only information was a slip of paper with the name Alexandria Hodgeman printed on it. The sisters determined that this was my name, and that's how I was addressed from then on. But I began to realize quite soon that this name wasn't equivalent to other girls' names; it wasn't short like Ann, Betty, or Mary; it was distinctive, but actually it was *too* distinctive. As a result I began experimenting with my name and shortening it to other forms.

The name Alexandria is actually the feminine version of Alexander, the name of rulers of at least seven different countries according to the encyclopedia I looked in. Alexandra was used by a woman in Russia. Names of men often have feminine counterparts; for example, William results in Willa, Wilhelmina, or Billie. John gives us Johnna, Johanna, Joan, or Joanna; even David can be made over to Davida.

I tried various names including Alex, but even though that had the advantage of being short and easy for people to say, it did sound like a boy's name. Alexander wasn't acceptable because that was surely a man's name. Andria sounded feminine enough, but that I rejected. Alexis seemed quite evocative, even sexy, but I wasn't certain I was an Alexis.

Finally, I settled on Alexandria as my name. Of course, my classmates insisted on using shortened versions of it which I accepted at times; some even called me Al which to me sounded like the name of a taxicab driver. Alex became my informal name which I didn't mind overly. However, if I felt testy I insisted that they use my complete name.

It was my name, and despite its demands on the speaker, I grew into it and became proud of it.

The closest anyone else's name came to the complications of Alexandria was Elizabeth. There are numerous variations of this name including Liz, Beth, Liza, and even Lisabeth. The most effective queen of England was Elizabeth I, so that is a name to wear with pride. But there are numerous choices for someone named Elizabeth.

I suppose as a result of my name being somewhat out of the ordinary, I began to think about names and to analyze them more than most people do. I have heard of people being named Petersele or Hogg, which I suppose is nothing the owners could control, but they certainly could control the names chosen for their offspring. What sensitive parent with the name Hogg would name a daughter Ima, for example? I always thought these parents must have hated their children. Couldn't they expect the children to repay them some time for imposing such names onto them?

The sisters of Mercy insisted that every one of us girls have a middle name taken from a saint which was a patronym. The theory, evidently, was that such naming would cause us to emulate the saint we were named after. There were dozens to choose from, of course, as the book of saints is a massive compendium of all the martyrs and saints. Teresa and Mary were quite popular, but Ruth, Esther, Bernadette, Rachel, Therese and many others were used. My middle name, used only by the sisters or the priest, was Leah. In the Old Testament, Leah was the first wife of Jacob and the mother of six of Jacob's sons, but she wasn't loved by Jacob. She was called "tender-eyed" which might refer to her poor vision.

When we studied poetry, I discovered that my name had three natural stresses: Alex-AN-dria, LE-ah HODGE-man. In that way, it had some beauty, I felt, as poetry seemed to speak to me sometimes more than prose.

The sisters all had taken different names once they became nuns. In some orders, they were all required to take Mary as their first name, but this wasn't true of the sisters of Mercy. We had sister Mary, sister Elizabeth, and sister Zipporah. There was even sister Steve; I never saw why a sister had to take a man's name, but I suppose that name referred to St. Stephen.

After these eighty-nine years I have become quite comfortable with my name. There are people who don't like their names, I know. Some even go to court to have their names changed. I have never understood how a person could do that. How could you sacrifice your identity that way, for we do become our names? If we live with them long enough, we become them. What sort of chameleon could just drop her name and become someone else? Wouldn't that require re-inventing self, becoming a new person? This was a challenge of marriage, too. I never had to consider changing my name to that of a husband, so I'm not certain what I'd have done. I might have resisted. Or I might have hyphenated my name as some modern women have done. Why should I sacrifice my identity to that of someone else's? Shouldn't the sacrament of marriage recognize both parties as being equivalent and equal? The days of male superiority were gone, I thought. Rarefied thinking, perhaps, but I guess I have become a liberated woman.

Chapter Four

On a cold, winter's morning, the Sisters of Mercy assembled all of us who had reached the age of reason for a presentation. The little children were excused, but all of us past the third grade were required to attend.

Sister Margarita stood at the front of the room. She seemed tall and daunting to me, an avatar of threat. We all knew of her bent to punishment; she seemed to enjoy punishing us. Maybe she didn't actually enjoy punishing us, but I thought there was a cast in her eye that revealed a devilish enjoyment which I didn't wish to be on the receiving end of.

"Girls, I need to talk to you today about sin." I could feel a tightening of personalities around the room. Never did we get talked to about pleasure or happiness; no, sin was a common topic with the sisters, and Sister Margarita was evidently the resident expert.

"I'm certain you all know the difference between venial and mortal sins, so I won't repeat that. What I'm talking about is men."

She paused to let us examine the word and bring to bear on it our own definitions.

"And boys. For boys grow up to become men." One of the girls behind me giggled but stopped abruptly, realizing where she was.

"I do not see that this is a matter to be laughed at." She glared at us, daring us to laugh, even to snicker or smile. None of us did. We were sufficiently cowed that we might have been Lot's wife after her transformation.

"Boys and men are after only one thing. They want your bodies.

And what you have to do is protect yourself. Your virginity—your purity—is the most valuable part of your existence that you have. You must bring yourselves to Jesus as pure as the driven snow with no blot or sin.

"All of the sisters here know what men are like, but you don't. You must listen to us and never—*never* give in to men's pleadings and demanding. For what they want is to plunge you into the deepest, darkest abyss of sin—to use you, and then to cast you aside. They want to take your beautiful, pure bodies and defile them. To defile them until you become as ugly as Satan. And only then will they be satisfied. Only then will they smile and enjoy their dirty work.

"It will be a life's work for every one of you to protect yourself against men. I'm not talking about white slavers—although you must guard against them, of course. I'm referring to the everyday men you meet at the drug store or at the motion pictures. Some even go to church. Yes, they go to church, looking for their victims, because they are truly doing the work of the Devil. You must protect yourself.

"How do you do this? By avoiding the places where these men can seduce you. They talk sweetly, they buy you alcohol, offer you cigarettes, encourage you to wear lipstick and perfume, and the next thing you know, they are enjoying your bodies. Girls, you have been give a precious gift from God that you must not defile. You must protect yourself from visiting any place where a man can take advantage of you. For they will try. Oh, they will strive mightily to remove your clothing, to gaze upon your naked bodies, and then to defile you. At such a time you must remember Saint Teresa who lived a life of pure submission, enduring endless pain, but who never gave in to sin. Think of the martyrs with hundreds of arrows piercing their beautiful bodies who died pure in mind and body. Some suffered crucifixion, but none of then yielded to sin. You must be strong. You must not sacrifice your purity."

The room was extremely quiet. There was no shuffling, sneezing, or coughing which was itself a surprise considering the temperature and the weather—gray and overcast. But above the silence I could feel thinking in the room. "What about husbands? Are they dirty, too? Are they meant to entice us into sin? What about marriage?"

As if Sister Margarita had heard these thoughts, she went on. "Not all men are like this. My father is a wonderful man. I mean my father before I became a sister. Some of you will marry and bear children. But even then you must protect yourself against sinful occasions. There is no earthly reason that your husband should ever see you naked. You must protect your modesty. You must keep your body covered, for too much freedom becomes license to sin. And we all know we have to avoid sin."

Sister Margarita faced us all defiantly. "I urge all of you to pledge yourselves to leading a life of purity, free from sin, free from defilement, and free from temptation. Above all, you must avoid temptation."

We waited, but evidently there was nothing more to be added. Sister Margarita stood erectly without adding anything further. Finally, we were dismissed to return to our classrooms and to try to decipher the meaning of Sister Margarita's warning.

Chapter Five

Life at the Sisters of Mercy Orphanage was tolerable, even if it wasn't what I might have wished for myself. Actually since I had no basis of comparison, I found that I could abide whatever came my way and not be overly disappointed.

From an early age all of us girls were given chores. Even the smallest children were expected to help out, even if it was no more than running a dust cloth over the pews in the church.

After I began grade school, the sisters tried me at various jobs; one which I liked more than some of the others was working in the kitchen. At least there I was in contact with food. We were given food that was meant to sustain us in our daily lives, but there was no food that would lead anyone to hymns of exaltation, and often there wasn't enough to fill us up. Most of the food was functional only; whatever decorative touches were added had to be added by those of us who were consuming it as the cooks did nothing more than mix it, bake or fry it, and serve it. If someone wanted swirls in her mashed potatoes, she had to add the swirls herself.

The one cook I remember most notably is Mrs. Breame. She was somewhat taller than the sisters, and she looked as if she never ate anything but string beans. I'm not certain why I remember her more than any of the others, except that she made a strong impression on me of never being satisfied or pleased with anything. Her face had grown into a perpetual downturn which on most people would be seen as a frown, but I think Mrs. Breame wasn't actually frowning; I think it was just her natural expression. Perhaps she found the world wanting or everything was distasteful to her, but I cannot recall that I ever saw her smile, let alone laugh. She went about the business of cooking with an intensity that brooked no interference from anyone. This attitude was most notable immediately before a meal was to be served. She had a job to do, and anybody who interfered with her performing that job would suffer.

Once the food was finished and available to be served from the lines as the girls filed through, she appeared to relax modestly, standing and supervising those of us who served the various casseroles or boiled vegetables.

We seemed to live on macaroni and cheese, especially on Holy Days of Obligation and Wednesdays and Fridays when meat was not permitted. Of course, we ate beans regularly, too. Once in a while there was meat, but it was always a small portion, not even a child's size that one would get at a restaurant today. Usually it was a meat loaf with plenty of filler to stretch the meat.

I had been working in the kitchen serving food and washing dishes for several years when it occurred to me one day that I had never seen Mrs. Breame taste anything she was making.

"How do you know if it's any good if you don't taste it?" I asked.

"The recipe."

"What if the recipe's wrong?"

"Impossible." She gave a bit of shake to her head at such a notion.

"What if the ingredients are bad?"

This stopped her momentarily. Then she answered, "Somebody will tell me." Of course, this was so. Not the students, of course. We all knew better than to complain about the food. Those who might complain or—heaven forbid—ask for more were dressed down immediately by either Mrs. Breame or one of the sisters. We had heard of Oliver Twist, and his example was used to keep us thankful and not asking for more. The result was that oftentimes we were hungry, but we certainly weren't overweight.

I suppose one of the sisters might have informed Mrs. Breame that the dish wasn't exactly right if the ingredients weren't good, but I can't remember that ever happening.

It is uncharitable of me, I see now, but Mrs. Breame never caused any feelings in me except distaste. And, of course this was wrong, especially as she was a cook. I ate what she fixed, and often it was good—especially considering what she had to work with and the restrictions on budget—but how could anyone cook a dish without tasting it?

Later on after I moved into the boarding house, I saw Mrs. Watson cook as I occasionally helped her get food onto the table; she enjoyed cooking. Of course she had the figure to go with it, too, being slightly overweight. She had a matching disposition, too, enjoying food and enjoying people, perpetually smiling and exhorting people to eat up. She always tasted her food as she prepared it.

Others saw Mrs. Breame in the same light, I suspect, for behind her back, they called her String Bean. That was natural as she did resemble that vegetable.

All of the girls who worked in the kitchen were required to wear hair nets. This was to keep our hair out of the food. We had to follow other rules of hygiene, too, such as always wearing a clean apron and washing our hands before we helped serve. This was decades before food servers were required to pass a test. There were no gloves to be worn either, but we were discouraged from touching the food with our hands.

Some of the girls wore jewelry which interfered with their work in the kitchen. As a result they always had to remove it. In fact the sisters discouraged wearing any jewelry at all except for the ring they wore signifying their marriage to Christ. Earrings, necklaces, and bracelets might fall into the food, so if anyone did wear such decorations, she had to remove them before serving.

Almost all of the girls loved jewelry. I'm not certain why. There was something about flashing earrings, for example, that most of them loved. Some even pierced their ears which was forbidden, but they ignored the sisters' warnings about infections and, using a heated needle, pierced each others' lobes, pulling a thread back and forth through the hole until it healed, leaving a place to attach some bit of stone or flashy color.

I tried to like jewelry. I admired the pretty colored stones or glass and even envied them but, when finally I had a bracelet of my own, I didn't like it on me. For some reason the very feeling irritated me, and I couldn't wait to take it off. Later on, after I bought a wristwatch, I found that it, too, made me uncomfortable. Finally I traded it for a pendant watch which didn't touch my skin.

Later on Edward and I talked about rings for each other, but I wasn't enthusiastic about wearing a ring. I know today that men want to own women, and one way of staking their claim is with a ring, not through the nose—that's too primitive—but with rings on the fingers. I couldn't abide a ring or anything else hanging on me. Since we didn't have extra money at that time, we never got rings, and then he was shipped out.

This lack of appreciation for jewelry may be another reason I have always been perceived as plain—in fact, that's the way I see myself—just plain old me.

Today, being eighty-nine, I suppose I could wear anything I wanted, and nobody would care. I've read about the red hat societies made up of women who wear red hats and purple clothing right out in public. I suppose this is one way of their making a statement of their independence, but what sort of independence is it that requires someone to make a public statement? Isn't being independent enough by itself without having to proclaim it? At my age, I guess I don't have to proclaim anything.

Chapter Six

Oh, despite my religious training and upbringing I've known a man. I should be ashamed of it as we didn't marry and I let him use my body. But what did I care? What's a woman's body for except to make babies, and why can't a woman enjoy the pleasure of that act as well as a man? A hussy I'd be called by some, and I suppose they would be right, but I knew in my heart, just as much as I knew that Sister Aimee was a good person doing God's work, that Edward was the man for me.

The problem was he didn't know it, himself, at least at first, and there was no way I could make him see it. I met him when I was eighteen, still working at the bookstore and caring for books with heart and soul, and not realizing that there was an ache in my heart which needed soothing. We women are strong when it comes to denying ourselves. I've seen it in others, and I've noted it in myself after the fact. Not when the thing is happening, naturally, but later on I'll see the truth of it.

He had been away from home, so I hadn't seen him before when one afternoon he stopped in to ask about a book "Oh, hello," he said to me. "Who are you?"

"My name is Alexandria. I manage the bookstore."

He studied me for a moment. "Do you like your work?"

"Oh, yes; I wouldn't do anything else. Are you looking for a book?"

"Maybe. Do you have any?"

"Hundreds. Why don't you look around?"

I got busy, and then he was gone before I could even appreciate him.

The joy of it, however, was that he returned for books regularly or maybe just to see me, and as we got to know each other, he began to stay a few moments. Foolishly I began to look forward to seeing him, anticipating a friendly greeting or smile. Occasionally, he offered some little joke meant only for me, and I thought that he was beginning to take to me. I hoped so as he had already captured my heart.

Edward Carmody had been away to college and was home for the summer, working to earn money so he could afford to return. He was taller than I, close to six feet and nicely proportioned. In those days, very few men were overweight as they have become today, and I imagined his body would be sleek and strong.

He had coal black hair which he was somewhat negligent about, pushing it out of his eyes occasionally as he talked to me. I noticed that if the air was heavy with moisture or if it was raining, his hair curled. When I asked him about it once, he complained, "Oh, yes, when it rains my hair curls up almost as if I'd been to a beauty shop for a wash and set." I laughed.

Despite my natural reservations and hesitation, there developed a place in me—perhaps in my heart—that thrilled whenever Edward Carmody showed up. He seemed like such a desirable man that I knew I could never have a chance of being anything more than a speaking acquaintance of his.

And he was smart. He was to be a senior when he returned to college, and already he knew a great deal. When I asked him what he was studying, he answered, "I will be an English teacher."

He said that so fiercely, that I wondered why. "Oh, my mother isn't pleased with me for wanting to be a teacher; teachers don't earn much, you know, but that is what I must be. I want to teach."

I was surprised and pleased when Edward invited me to share a cup of coffee or tea one afternoon with him. I explained that I wasn't free except for Sundays. "How about after church, then?" he asked. "We could share the afternoon."

I thought about that while my heart was racing. "I suppose that would be all right," I finally said.

He looked at me somewhat skeptically. "If you don't want to, you know, you don't have to."

"Oh, no. I want to. I just don't want you to have to spend money on me."

"Alexandria, I want to. It isn't every day I get to spend time with a beautiful, young woman."

For a moment I suspected he was making fun of me or at least teasing me. Never had I considered that I was beautiful. But hopefully, I decided to take it as a compliment.

"I'd love to spend the afternoon with you," I said.

The days until we were to meet raced by on wings of angels or slowed down to the measured pace of turtles. When he came for me, I couldn't remember dealing with anyone or of thinking of anything but him. When I stepped outside myself, I began to see why a woman would choose to give herself to a man. The sisters had warned us, of course. "Never give in to a man," they had said repeatedly, and of course all of us girls at the Sisters of Mercy accepted their warning. But they had forgotten to tell us of the thrill of watching a young man's eyes light up just on seeing us, or the excruciating pleasure of being the center of attention of a handsome young man who was focusing on us alone. More likely they didn't know. Probably the sisters had been so focused on Jesus Christ that they had never even seen the potential for shared love with a man. I began to suspect that if they had, their advice to us wouldn't have been so vociferous or so laden with potential danger.

What I ate I don't remember. After we walked in the park, Edward took me to a neighborhood café where we could eat satisfying food for only twenty-five cents. We talked about our lives so far and what we hoped for the future. I told Edward that I loved books and wanted to continue to work with them.

"What about children?" he asked. "Have you ever thought of having babies of your own?"

"Of course, I have. But that is for the future with the right person."

"Yes. Marriage is an important step."

I had thought of marriage, but I had discounted it as I had thought no man would ever want to marry me. What did I have to offer? I wasn't beautiful, I had no family or status, and my upbringing and education were minimal at best. Dowries were not the custom in the United States, and a good thing for me, too, since there would be no dowry.

Yet as far as I could tell, Edward was content to wait. The future would come, whatever he and I did, and there was no need to rush it.

At the end of that summer, Germany invaded Poland, and everyone said it was the beginning of a world war. People were still getting over the war which had ended in 1918, and now it appeared that there was to be war again. When I asked Edward about it, he said, "The United States cannot be dragged into this. It is Europe's battle, and we have to let them solve their own problems."

There was a great strain of isolationism in the United States in those days, so I wasn't surprised or dismayed by what he said.

The next spring he was graduated from college and almost immediately he was hired to teach ninth grade in a high school. When he told me about being hired, he could hardly contain himself. "Finally, I'll get to see whether I'm a teacher or not," he said. "I can hardly wait." It was exciting for me, too, just to see his immoderate enthusiasm; anyone could see that he was eager to be tested. I felt he would not be found wanting.

The high school was not far from where I was living with Mrs. Watson in southern California, so it became usual for Edward to call for me on Friday night. His school week was over, and he could relax as he had time before having to grade papers over the weekend. I grew accustomed to listening to him regale me with his adventures in the classroom. They truly were adventures. I suspect that with other teachers they would just be daily occurrences not to be made much of, but with him they were to be savored and treasured, shared and laughed over.

Still, even though I shared his joys and triumphs, I began to feel a sense of unease. I truly wanted him, and I believed we should marry. How else could I experience true womanhood, even have babies? Yet, despite my impatience, I saw that he couldn't be rushed. Maybe after he had taught for a year he would be ready to act.

What was hard was the sexual urges which began to take over my body and captivate my mind. I knew he wanted my body as we kissed with abandon, sitting on the verandah of Mrs. Watson's. At first, the kisses were somewhat tentative and exploratory, but as we grew to know each other more fully and the pleasure heightened, it was almost impossible to resist going on. The time of the kisses lengthened, and he began to explore my body with his hands. I knew I should stop him, but truthfully I enjoyed having him touch me with his hands exploring my body. I felt myself come alive with desire which seemed to permeate my whole existence right down to my soul, and I wanted him as much as I had ever wanted anything in my life. Still, the training of the sisters was so strong that I held out. I allowed him to fondle me through my clothing but only above the waist. When he made gestures of reaching beneath my blouse or sweater, I stopped him, saying, "No," and he always stopped. Probably he wouldn't have if he had known how much my body ached to have him continue. I wanted to feel his body against mine, and it took every ounce of restraint and resolve in me to keep from baring my body and asking him to kiss me all over.

How long we could have continued to behave like this—tantalizing each other and torturing each other—I don't know. But it all ended the summer before Pearl Harbor was attacked when he decided he had to enlist in the U.S. Navy. We argued about it, naturally, as I didn't want him to go. "What about your teaching? You've had only one year; that isn't enough."

"No, it isn't. But I have to do this. Don't you see, the United States will have to get into the war some time, and I want to be part of this. I can always teach after the war."

His boot camp was in San Diego, so we weren't far apart, but despite his being near, there was an increased distance between us. In a way I felt I had been deserted. Yes, that was selfish on my part, but I couldn't change so easily. I didn't want to lose him, and I was deathly afraid that I might.

After boot camp, Edward came home on leave. I knew he would be shipping out, and I knew he might not come back. So I went to a hotel downtown and booked a room for the weekend. When Edward came for me on Friday night, I didn't let on that I had planned anything different. We shared supper and talked about where he might go. Of course we swore to write to each other.

After we finished eating, I told him I wanted him to take me to the hotel. "What for? Why?" he asked.

"Edward."

He stared at me for a moment, wondering, I suppose. Then he smiled and nodded his head. "Okay. Okay, if this is what you want. It is what you want, isn't it?"

"Yes."

I haven't shared details about any of this with other women, so I don't know what their experiences were like, but for me, that weekend was the epitome of sharing of self. I had decided we would do it, and this was the time. There was some initial pain, but he was so gentle and loving that it was sweet pain, and after that we simply pleasured ourselves. He kissed my body with abandon and after I got used to the notion, I kissed him all over, too. It was total pleasure to discover his body just as I had imagined it, and he took such pleasure in me that I couldn't regard what we did as a sin, despite what the sisters of Mercy would say.

Having experienced that weekend, I understand completely how a woman might give up everything for a man, even knowing that he might be worthless and might betray her. If she felt anything like what I felt, she wouldn't hesitate a second. I felt great joy that apparently Edward felt the same way about me.

We agreed to marry, but both of us saw it didn't have to be right away. I think we were both confident that our love would be enough to sustain us.

After Edward shipped out, we exchanged letters—letters filled with our daily activities which danced around true complete expressions of our commitment and signed with predictable statements of love. But I knew as I read his letters and I hoped he knew as he read mine that our true feelings were so much more than what the letters expressed that it was impossible to express in writing what we felt. I looked forward to his letters as I assumed he anticipated mine, as opportunities to re-connect and to re-establish our communion.

Truthfully, I wasn't prepared for the telegram. Since Edward had listed me as his next of kin, I was notified officially. The ship had been sunk, not at Pearl Harbor but afterwards. I had fleetingly considered that he might be lost to me, but that unbidden thought I had banished to a closed vault in my mind, never to be brought out into direct sunlight.

Yes, I grew used to the thought that I would never see him again. Although it had already been months, I still entertained some forlorn hope that I might be pregnant with his child, but that was not to be. Later on when I read A. J. Cronin's *The Citadel* I saw how somebody else dealt with grief. For me, life plodded wearily on, and eventually I was no longer disappointed that the mail didn't reward me with word from him.

I think it took until after the war for me to finally accept that I would never enjoy such a transcendent connection again. Occasionally, I might see a young man and admire his physique, but the thought was always fleeting; never did I entertain the notion of pursuing a physical connection with another man. I had enjoyed something reverent and almost spiritual with Edward, and to try to re-visit it with someone else would be to profane it. His memory sustains me yet today.

Chapter Seven

It's challenging to me to summarize my life or to conclude what I have learned. Of course, I have picked up certain bits of knowledge along the way, but if anyone asked me to be profound about it, I couldn't be. When Dorothy Gale is asked, "What have you learned?" in *The Wizard of Oz*, she answers that she has learned to look in her own back yard. The answer she gives is somewhat facile, almost as if she had it prepared before-hand. This is certainly not true of me. But there are a few bits I have accrued over the years which may, in their modest ways, be gems of wisdom.

When I was a girl at the Sisters of Mercy, I lacked a family. Somewhere out there was a mother and surely a father, too, but I never got to see them. Some of the girls had families who came to visit them. They had been placed with the sisters as a temporary solution to money problems or living arrangements, and in time they were re-claimed by their families. I knew this wouldn't happen to me.

One item that summarized this lack in me was the fact that I didn't have a family bible, that my name wasn't written down for someone to read. Somehow it seemed that if my name had been recorded and people could read it aloud, my existence would be proved or justified. I had read about families who had bibles with everybody's name inscribed. And I wished I had a family bible with my name written in it. I wanted a family and I wanted an acknowledgement of my existence. Without a family bible, I didn't seem to be real. Not knowing my actual birth date was only part of it.

Somehow I needed affirmation of myself. I always thought a bible would give me that. Probably it wouldn't have, but I knew there was something missing from my life: some affirmation or definition that wasn't obvious but which was still a hole or a gap in my personality. It was as if there was an absence which needed to be filled. I had seen a tree cut down which was diseased, so it had to be removed. After it was gone, I still felt its presence, and whenever I passed by where it had been, I some way expected to see it again. Birds even flew to it, attempting to land on its missing branches, but it was no longer there. This hole in the sky seemed to be symbolic of the hole in my life which I just couldn't fill.

After I left the Sisters of Mercy, I began to make friends with women I worked with and people I met at the boarding house. After I bought my house, I met my neighbors, and it was natural that we exchange telephone numbers. I carefully recorded people's names, addresses, and telephone numbers in a free address book that Mr. Skolnik gave me. And for years I was careful about making certain I had current information about everyone.

But as I've gotten older, I realized something about address books. When we're young, we're never told about the betrayal of address books. We get our first address book and diligently and faithfully record the names, addresses, and telephone numbers of everyone. When that book is full, or too frayed to use again, we transfer the names to another booklet and make sure to do it in pencil this time. Do we just discard the old address book?

Then time catches up with us, and we have to decide what to do with names and addresses which are no longer valid. Do we cross them off? I couldn't do that. Death is bad enough. Crossing people off would be equivalent to removing them from our lives and our memories. So I leave them. Their names become stark reminders of what once was.

In a way the address book becomes a rebuke to me for living. I see the names—some almost forgotten—and remember and regret. Address books are our archeological digs—of past life and lives, of past friendships, even relatives.

I can't abide looking through my address book for long. Not only does it make me sad, but it also reminds me of lost opportunities. At eighty-nine years of age, I've experienced many lost opportunities. Even though I've had my memories of Edward to savor all these years, sometimes the memories seem so evanescent and delicate that they hardly exist anymore. Did we really have what I think we did? And was I wrong to hold onto those in place of seeking out someone else? Surely I could have had additional opportunities, men being what they are.

When I worked part-time in the book store, it would have been easy for me to encourage a man. There are certain looks or even glances that signal a man's interest. But I didn't want to replace the memories of Edward with any other experiences, so maybe I settled for less. At the time it didn't seem like less. In fact, I thought I had experienced the very best that was available. But today, maybe I'm not so certain. After these more than seventy years, I doubt myself at times.

The problem with any relationship is that one has to be willing to take chances, to extend self into the other's person's world or admit him or her into yours, and sometimes we misjudge others. It's possible that the other person's motives may not be the same as ours; some people are inconsiderate and even hateful. The problem with admitting someone like that into your life is that often it's not possible to know until it's too late. Then what? The relationship is not healthy; in fact, it's damaged or faulty. And how does one go about repairing a flawed relationship?

It's as if one could imagine a faulty relationship like a broken car, maybe a faulty vacuum cleaner. So all you have to do is open it up, take out the defective parts, and replace them; then it will run like new. But a relationship isn't repairable that way. There are parts of a relationship that can't be replaced. Once they're worn out, they're gone. There is no fixing there. Not only that, but some relationships are never meant to be repaired. When they're gone, it's over. All you can do is move on. Still I must confess that I have my doubts, and I suppose they might even be termed regrets. I was never so certain in my life that I always knew I was doing the right thing.

Perhaps this doubt is a sign of the need for a connection to something higher, something that transcends our everyday existence. I never found it at the Sisters of Mercy, but then I was too young then, and what the sisters knew of religion and a higher authority was imposed onto us—we had no choice.

Maybe that's why Sister Aimee spoke so definitively to me. Maybe that's why I heard her voice so loud and clear. I'm not a fundamentalist or a holy roller, but when Sister Aimee spoke it seemed as if she might be speaking directly to me, and I wanted to be the same as she was: someone who knew her way and was willing to lead others. Long after Sister Aimee's death, I continued to feel that need in my life and, in fact, I think it's still with me today. I guess it's a basic need for connection which transcends our relationships with people. Perhaps Jesus gave that to the apostles; at least that's what it appears to be in the New Testament. But truthfully, I still haven't resolved this to my satisfaction.

Chapter Eight

It was hard to separate the truth from fiction during the days when Sister Aimee was at her peak. It was said that the Angelus Temple had cost $1,500,000 to build in 1923; this was an unheard of sum. Even during the roaring 20s, this was more money than most people could imagine.

On top of the temple was a rotating lighted cross which it was said could be seen from fifty miles away. There was the radio station, too, which broadcast the "Foursquare Gospel" around the world. It was reported that there was a special "Miracle Room" which featured stacks of crutches, wheelchairs, and braces left after people had been cured.

What I liked about the broadcasts is that Sister Aimee wasn't so fearful or threatening. Instead she seemed to be comforting. Rather than focus on hell, Sister Aimee offered the pleasures of heaven. I know the broadcasts didn't do her justice, but I could just imagine what it was like. With her beautiful hair and dressed all in white, I knew Sister Aimee would be a sight to behold.

One of her sermons was called "Throw Out the Lifeline." This featured a dozen young women, virgins all, dressed in white, clinging desperately to a Rock of Ages. This was accompanied by all the sounds of nature: thunder, wind, and occasional flashes of lightning. This went on for a few minutes until people could hardly stand the suspense. Then out would come Sister Aimee dressed in an admiral's uniform with a company of lady sailors. They threw out the blessed lifeline while a male chorus, dressed as coastguard men, swept the mechanical waves with searchlights. The virgins were saved, the music rose to a crescendo, and the congregation cheered. Over it all waved the American flag.

I had not seen "Throw Out the Lifeline," but I could certainly imagine it. How spectacular it must have been. Sister Aimee inspired me just with her words; in person I'm sure it would have been grand and glorious.

In a way, I suppose Sister Aimee had thrown out the lifeline to me because when I listened to the broadcasts, I hung on her every word; it seemed as though she was talking directly to me. I felt that if I ever had a lifeline, it would come from Sister Aimee. Listening to one of her broadcasts offered me reassurance that I didn't seem to derive from any other source. I felt she was the epitome of salvation.

Chapter Nine

I met Mr. Skolnik one day as I walking along, not minding where I was going, looking into shop windows. Then I realized I was in front of a window that was filled with books. I had seen a reference to *Moby Dick*, so I decided to buy it.

In the store it was murky and smelled of tobacco and smoke. Behind a counter was a gray-haired man who looked up, questioningly. "You want a book maybe?" he asked.

"Yes; *Moby Dick*."

"That's a book?"

"Yes. By Melville; Herman Melville."

"This book I don't know. You want something else?"

"No. I want *Moby Dick*."

"Ain't got him. Something else."

"It is a very famous book. You must have it. It's about whaling."

"Oh." His eyes lit up. "Whaling, I got." He stood up and walked to a shelf. I saw he was rather short and a bit overweight, but he moved purposefully to a shelf, reached out, and pulled down a book. Then he brought it back to the counter and laid it in front of me. I saw it was *Moby Dick*.

"But this is what I asked for. This is *Moby Dick*."

"Ain't got. This is a book on whaling."

"Yes, *Moby Dick* is about whaling."

"Whaling I got. No *Moby Dick*."

Somehow he knew the contents of the book but not the title. I bought it and read it.

The next time I went back, I asked for *The Adventures of Huckleberry Finn*.

"That's a book?" he asked.

"Yes, a very famous book by Mark Twain."

"No. Ain't got him. Something else?"

"It's all about a boy's adventures rafting down the Mississippi."

"Ah. Mississippi rafting." He stood up, shuffled over to a shelf, removed a book, and brought it back. It was *The Adventures of Huckleberry Finn*.

"But this is what I asked for. This is *The Adventures of Huckleberry Finn*."

"No. Ain't got. Got book of rafting on the Mississippi."

Eventually after I got acquainted with him—his name was Mr. Skolnik—I realized his grasp of English wasn't complete. Titles eluded him, and even though he could make out the books, he didn't retain the titles. He remembered them based on their contents. After that when I wanted a specific book, all I had to do was ask for it by content. Nearly always Mr. Skolnik could go immediately to the shelf to get the book I wanted.

Chapter Ten

When I was working part-time at the book store, one morning I woke up from a painful dream. I've read that dreams are products of our own mind, of what we are thinking, so to some extent we are responsible for our dreams, but this one I could find no basis for. In the dream I was tied up with ropes and chains, in handcuffs, and my feet were immersed in mire, which was thick and grasping, the texture of oatmeal or porridge, so that I could hardly move. Obviously the dream was the result of some sense of constraint or restraint but beyond that I couldn't fathom it. What was it that was holding me back? Was it my life?

I noted also that my jaws were sore as if I had been clenching them. The dream left me feeling adrift as if I had no sense of my direction or purpose. Where *was* I going in my life? I couldn't answer this question. Shaken and disturbed, I got out of bed to make a cup of tea. As the water heated, I sat at my dresser which I used as a table and asked myself what lay in the future? I didn't know.

From the Sisters of Mercy I had gone to cleaning and washing, and from there I went on to the book store. None of the work I did was important to anyone except to me, and then only because the pay helped me support myself. Shouldn't life be more than just working for wages? I felt there ought to be more.

When the water was ready, I poured it over some tea leaves and watched them gradually swirl and color the water. As I waited for the leaves to settle, I inhaled the peaceful and settling aroma of the tea itself. I had long admired Sister Aimee, but I simply couldn't envision myself serving as she did. It appeared to me that to work as she did required a much more aggressive and outgoing personality than I possessed. In addition, there probably should be some connection to God, some drive or call as people refer to it.

This wasn't the only time I had suffered from a disturbing dream. Some years earlier, just after I left the Sisters of Mercy, I had waked up about 3:30 in the morning on the verge of screaming. In my dream a man with an axe or hatchet had been about to attack some children, and I was where I could see this, but there was nothing I could do to prevent him. Such horror was excruciating to me, and it took me several minutes to regain my balance. Even then I saw how much I loved children, and to be helpless in the face of tragedy was immobilizing. Maybe my future lay in working with children, in helping them in some way. This thought attracted me as I saw that if I could bring it about, I would probably be much more at peace with myself while simultaneously helping others. It was at that moment, that I set out on the path which would eventually bring me very satisfying and enriching work.

I suppose I've always known I would never have children, would never birth babies, would never nurture them at my breast. I knew it would require a man, and truly I wanted no man using my body, even to create a baby, especially after Edward. Yet despite this knowing, there was a sense of wanting, of desire, which needed the touch of a new hand, the glance of a fresh eye which might serve to liberate me—to set me free of this world and all of its gravity which continues to weigh everyone down.

Wanting children but not wanting the conditions, what was I to do? If I couldn't be a mother literally, perhaps I could mother children for others. And why not? Surely the pleasure of children's innocence is not restricted to their parents. Why couldn't I enjoy this, too, even at a remove? God's world is immense, more than I can see, and it must include more than just cleaning bathrooms and making beds or selling used books. Children I would have, and God would be served. This I knew.

There was something else, too. Children seemed to understand me and I understood them. Adults? I don't remember when it first occurred to me, but one day I saw I was invisible to adults. I could be in the same room, but it was almost as if I wasn't there. Unless I said or did something, people seemed not to see me. I was actually there, but there was no acknowledgement on others' parts.

This wasn't so with children. Children recognized me, maybe as one of them. They saw me and accepted me. But to adults I didn't exist. I might as well not have been there at all.

Chapter Eleven

After I left the Sisters of Mercy, my life changed. I had to focus on earning money, eating meals on my own, paying rent, and just getting along in life. I still tried to follow Sister Aimee, however. Whenever a story appeared in the newspaper, I read it and wondered how she was getting along and how the Angelus Temple was surviving during the depression. There were spiteful and hateful stories in the newspaper which I read but which I didn't really believe. Maybe Sister Aimee hadn't been kidnapped as people said, but I didn't entertain that thought. If she said she had, that was enough for me.

There was even a song about Sister Aimee called "The Ballad of Aimee McPherson." It was uncomplimentary, telling about her disappearance and linking her to a man named Ormiston or Armistad who ran her radio station.

Another story came from Milton Berle who said he had had an affair with Sister Aimee in 1930. Evidently he supplied details to try to make his story convincing, but I didn't believe it. In fact, some of the details appeared to be either manufactured or false. Sister Aimee had been ill during the time when Berle said they got together, and I just couldn't imagine Sister Aimee behaving in such a way.

More and more the stories in the newspapers were critical, maybe because the writers felt some sort of betrayal. It's hard for me to say. After her marriage to David Hutton, I thought maybe now she would get back on track and rediscover her approach to salvation. Unfortunately, the marriage didn't work out. Two days after the wedding Hutton was sued for alienation of affection by Hazel St. Pierre. Hutton claimed he had never met her. Later it was reported that he paid her $5,000. This was during the depression, and $5,000 was enough to provide food for several families for a year. I guessed there must have been something to it for him to pay that much. When Sister Aimee heard about this, she fainted, fell, and hit her head on some flagstones.

Then while Aimee traveled in Europe, Hutton billed himself as "Aimee's man." He had a cabaret act which evidently needed something more to attract patrons.

In the church, the marriage wasn't welcomed either. According to the Foursquare Gospel which Sister Aimee had written, a person shouldn't remarry if a previous spouse was still alive. Aimee's was. Finally Sister Aimee and Hutton separated in 1933 and were divorced March 1, 1934.

After Aimee returned to Los Angeles, it was reported that fewer people were showing up at the Angelus Temple, but that I distrusted. I thought Sister Aimee was the same person as she had always been, and if others felt that way they wouldn't care what the newspapers said.

Then in 1936 Sister Aimee set out to help ease some of the problems caused by the Depression. She opened the temple commissary for twenty-four hours a day, seven days a week and helped to create soup kitchens and offer free medical assistance. Then when World War II began, she involved herself in war bond rallies, often using her sermons to link the church and Americanism. I was proud of Sister Aimee's patriotism.

Sister Aimee went to Oakland, California in 1944 to conduct some revivals featuring the "Story of My Life." On the morning of September 27, 1944, Rolf, her son, went to her hotel room where he found her unconscious. A half-empty bottle of Seconol capsules was discovered. She was pronounced dead by 11:15. There was an autopsy, but it wasn't definitive. Evidently Sister Aimee had been taking sleeping pills. Some people suggested that she had committed suicide, but I didn't believe that. Most people agreed with the coroner's report that it was an accidental overdose.

Sister Aimee was buried in Forest Lawn Memorial Park Cemetery in Glendale. There was a story going around that she was buried with an operating telephone, but I doubt that that was so.

Her son Rolf led the Foursquare Gospel church for forty-four years after her death, turning out to be a successful administrator even though he wasn't a revivalist like his mother. There had been a management dispute with his half-sister in 1936, but Rolf took Sister Aimee's side with the result that his sister lost the dispute and was removed from the church's leadership in 1937. She died in 2007 at age 96.

After Rolf took over leadership, the Foursquare movement grew from 29,000 members in 410 churches to 1.2 million members in 19,000 churches and worldwide meeting places by the time he retired.

By 2009 the church claimed to have over eight million members in 144 countries. Rolf retired in 1988 and died in 2009, also aged 96. KFSG had continued offering Christian radio broadcasts until it went off the air in 2003.

At my time in life I look back at Sister Aimee's life and her wonderful works, marveling at the great influence she exerted over people, healing people, and spreading God's word. At one time Sister Aimee was quoted as saying, "I am not a healer. Jesus is the healer. I am only the little office girl who opens the door and says, 'Come in.'" For someone to present herself so humbly, I think she had to have a very positive definition of herself and her purpose. I suppose it is possible that Sister Aimee was human just like the rest of us, guilty of the same trivial or petty behaviors, but I always wanted to see her as much more than that. To me she occupied an exalted position, and even if she was guilty of some of those sins she was accused of, she had a larger perspective than anybody else I ever encountered or read about in my life. For that alone I will not dishonor her memory.

Chapter Twelve

I discovered Mrs. Watson's quite by accident one afternoon as I was returning to the Sisters of Mercy having run an errand. One of the older women in the neighborhood had fallen and was confined to her bed, so the sisters had had soup delivered to her. She was a regular member of the congregation, but now she could no longer attend services.

A large, roomy house behind a picket fence standing about ten yards off the sidewalk caught my eye. It had two stories with a verandah out front and a fenced off balcony extending from the second floor. In the window of what might be the front room was a sign which proclaimed "Rooms to Rent." As I had just turned sixteen that spring, I was thinking ahead to the day when I could move out on my own. First, of course, I had to have a job, and jobs in 1937 were not easy to come by. In fact, many of the nation's workers were still out of work.

I'm not certain what prompted me to ask, but suddenly I resolved to find out what Mrs. Watson provided and what she charged. I walked up the three steps, opened the screen door into the verandah and crossed to the door where I twisted a manual-type bell which I could hear ring inside. Then the door was opened.

"Yes?" It was a woman of medium height, dressed neatly with an apron over her dress. I guessed she was middle-aged, but of that I couldn't be sure as it was impossible to guess the ages of the sisters, and I had very little experience with other women.

"I saw your sign," I said.

"The sign? Oh yes, about renting rooms. Well, I'm sorry, but I have no vacancies right now. I'm all full up. Actually, I'm not sorry at all. I'm glad. But I'm sorry that you had to ask when I have no rooms."

"Do you know when you might have a room?"

"Oh, no. People come and go. Today they have money, tomorrow they don't. And they have to pay rent. How long do you think I could stay here if I let people stay for nothing? Not very long, I'll tell you." Then she looked at me more carefully. "Why, you can't get a room, can you? You aren't old enough. How old are you?"

"I'm sixteen," I said with a trace of defiance.

"Oh. I thought you weren't—what am I doing? Please come in," she said, gesturing to invite me into the house. "I shouldn't keep you standing here. Come into the kitchen, and we'll have a cup of tea. You drink tea, don't you?"

"Yes," I answered, following her through the hallway and through a big room that I learned later was the dining room and into the kitchen. There was a table and chairs there and she gestured for me to sit down while she heated water.

"I usually have water on, but somehow I got distracted this afternoon so today I don't. It'll take only a minute." Then she sat down opposite me. "Now, tell me why you want a room. Is it for yourself?"

"Yes. You see, I just turned sixteen, and I should be getting out on my own soon. That is if I can find a job."

"Well, that's not so easy either, you know. Are you living at home?"

"Oh, no, I'm at the Sisters of Mercy Orphanage."

"Oh, you poor thing. No mother or father?"

"I suppose I do have, but I haven't met them yet."

She smiled. "Well, as I said I don't have a room available right now, but if one should open up, and you should get a job, then maybe we could come to an agreement. Now, the first thing I ask my prospective guests is, 'Do you smoke or drink?'"

I smiled. "No."

"Yes, I thought not. Do you keep late hours? You know I have six boarders here, and some of them have to get up early to go to work. They have to have their rest."

"No, I like to go to bed no later than ten o'clock."

"What about the radio? Do you have a radio which you play loud?"

"No, I don't own a radio."

"That's good. Well, I mean it's good that you don't have one so you can't play it loud. I suppose it would be good if you owned one and didn't play it loud. However, I have a radio in the parlor or dining room, and the boarders are free to listen to programs if they like. So long as they can agree on which programs. Sometimes, they don't agree, and then I have to be called in to settle it. Argue? You should hear them. You don't argue, do you?"

"No, I don't think so."

"No, well I wouldn't have thought you did." About then the tea kettle began to sing, and she got up to pour the tea. "After we've had our tea, I'll show you one of the rooms. In case one should open up, but as I said there's nothing right now. I hope you won't be disappointed."

"Oh, no, I couldn't move in right now anyway."

She brought out some homemade cookies to share and after she sat down told me bits of information about her boarders. She had been operating a boarding house for several years, since her husband had died. He had fought in the war and was gassed, so his health was never good after he returned from Europe.

"So after Henry died, I had to do something. Fortunately, the house was paid for, but still I couldn't live on nothing, could I? No. So after I thought about it, I decided I could rent out the rooms to single people. And that seems to work out fairly well."

"How much do you charge?"

"Well, you know I offer a light breakfast and supper in the evening. For that and the room I charge six dollars for single men and five dollars for single women. Per week. I think it's easier for men to pay the six dollars than it is for women to pay the five, don't you? You see, women can't get the same pay for jobs as men, and it's harder for them."

I nodded, wondering how I could find a job which would pay me five dollars a week. I had never had five dollars at one time in my life.

"What's your name? You haven't told me."

"Alexandria. Alexandria Hodgeman."

"Alexandria. My, what a beautiful name. And you have a beautiful face to go with it, too. What do people call you?"

"Alex, mostly."

"Alex. Do you like that?:"

"Oh, I don't mind. It is easier to say."

"Yes, it is. Alexandria. Makes me think of that town in Egypt. Founded by Alexander the Great, you know."

"Yes, I've read about it."

"I suppose you have. Wouldn't it be exciting to visit there? And maybe see the great library? Do you like libraries?"

"Yes, I do. I'm a reader."

"Oh, how wonderful. So am I, but I don't have the time to read as I used to when Henry was alive. But you know that library was destroyed by the Christians. What a loss that was. Manuscripts that can never be replaced. What a pity." She was silent for a moment. "Oh, my goodness, I haven't told you my name. My name is Mrs. Watson. Minnie is my first name, but everyone calls me Mrs. Watson, and I guess that's who I am after all these years. I used to be Minnie Colter, but after I got married I wasn't any longer. Isn't that strange? Don't you think so?"

"I suppose so—."

"Well, I mean that I just gave up my name, just like that, and became Mrs. Watson. You know some women don't do that. Every since women got suffrage, some women refuse to change their names. Nineteenth amendment, wasn't it?"

"Yes. Nineteen twenty."

"That's right. Nineteen twenty. And not a bit too soon, I think. How's your tea? Would you like another cookie?"

"No, thank you."

"Well, why don't we look into one of the rooms? Follow me." She led me into the hall off the dining room and up the stairs. The banister was smooth and shiny and I admired the wood as we climbed the carpeted stairs. At the top of the stairs, Mrs. Watson turned right and stopped to wait for me. "This is Mr. Kleinschmidt's room. He won't mind my showing you his room as he is extremely neat. He's one of the best roomers I have."

The door wasn't locked, and she opened it and stood aside so I could look around. To the left was a bureau with a mirror above it. There was a washbasin and pitcher atop the bureau. To the right of the bureau was a plain, straight-backed chair painted beige, and to the right of it was the bed. It was a single bed, I found out later, suitable for only one person. There was a headboard and just above it was a window which looked out over the balcony at the front of the house. To the right of the bed was a small closet.

"I won't open the closet," Mrs. Watson said. "That would be invading Mr. Kleinschmidt's privacy."

The room was small, but it was neat and tidy with everything arranged attractively. There was a carpet in front of the bed, but otherwise the floor was bare wood.

After giving me a moment to look around and to step over to the window, Mrs. Watson asked, "Well, what do you think? Do you think this would suit you?"

"I think it would," I answered, "if only I had a job."

"Well, that you'll have to see about. Come now, and I'll show you the bathroom."

The bathroom was at the end of the hall after two more closed doors on the right and three on the left. It had a sink, toilet, and a bathtub. The tub of porcelain stood on claw feet. I saw it would probably be luxurious to take a bath there. At the Sisters of Mercy we weren't permitted to indulge ourselves in a bath. Baths there were meant to wash the body and that was all.

I followed Mrs. Watson back downstairs where she showed me the dining room table. It was a long table with four straight-backed chairs on each side and a chair at the head and foot so it could seat ten in all. Against a wall stood a large floor model radio, the type I had seen in newspaper advertisements. There was also a shelf of books against the opposite wall.

"How many rooms do you have to rent?" I asked.

"Well, I have to let Jeannie have one, and then I have to have one, too—we're downstairs—so that leaves six in all."

"Eight rooms? My, this is a big house."

"Yes, but it wasn't always. I had some remodeling done after I began to rent out rooms."

"And the guests take their meals right here?"

"Oh, yes. Jeannie and I prepare the food and bring it in. We ring the bell when things are ready, and they come running. We serve good wholesome food. Not expensive, of course, but filling and appetizing.

Oh, the way some people eat. But I guess they're entitled to it as they're paying for it. But you don't want to come late to the table for a meal, I'll warn you. Might not be anything left." She smiled.

I liked Mrs. Watson and decided that if I could find work, I would try to get a room with her.

As I walked back to the Sisters of Mercy, I challenged myself on how to get a job. About all I was qualified for was cleaning and washing. But if that was what I had to do, I would do it. I had to get out on my own.

Chapter Thirteen

It was a bit of an accident that I began working at Books for Less run by Mr. Skolnik. In truth, it wasn't actually run by Mr. Skolnik. After I had visited his shop a time or two, I saw that he seemed to resent customers as they interfered with whatever he was doing; usually this was reading his Polish newspaper. Whenever anyone asked him for a particular book, his usual answer was, "Ain't got him." If the person insisted, he might rouse himself enough to check a shelf or two, but It was clear to me as I watched him that he wasn't enthusiastic and he didn't seem to care whether he found the book or not. Usually the customer became discouraged and left. I wondered whether he had any repeat business besides me.

One day I wandered into Books for Less to browse and maybe find something I might like to read. Books in those days were cheaper, of course, as we were still in the Depression, and I had hardly any income at the Sisters of Mercy. I was standing behind the first shelf which was close to the entrance when I heard someone ask for *Tom Sawyer*. "Ain't got him," Mr. Skolnik said.

"Oh, I can't believe that," the woman said. "It's a very famous book and quite popular, too. You must have it."

"Ain't got him," Mr. Skonik responded tonelessly, apparently uninterested in making any profit. I had just come across a copy of the book in the shelf below where I was looking, so I pulled the book off the shelf and took it to Mr. Skolnik.

"Here it is, Mr. Skolnik," I announced, handing it to him.

"Oh," he said. "Got him. Okay." He held it out to the woman.

"How much?" she asked.

"Oh, how much she wants to know. How much?" he asked me. I was nonplussed at first as I didn't really know the prices of books, but I had seen prices in a few of the books, and as this one was used, I suggested, "One dollar."

"One dollar? Isn't that high for a used book?" the woman asked.

"No, it isn't," I said. If you order it new, it might cost you $2.95 or even more. And this book is in good condition, too. Look. None of the pages is dog-eared, and it even has the book jacket."

Holding the book in her left hand, she riffled the pages, looking for signs of damage or underlining, I suppose. "Oh, all right. I'll take it. It's for my son's birthday. He'll be eleven next week." Laying the book onto the counter, she opened her purse, extracted a dollar bill, and handed it to me. "Thank you very much. I'm sure he will enjoy it."

Taking the dollar, I answered, "Oh, I'm sure he will. It's a great book."

"Oh, yes, I know. I've been reading Mark Twain for years. Did you know he wrote a book called *Life on the Mississippi*?"

"Yes. In fact, we have that on our shelf over here."

"Really? Well, if I ever want to own it, I'll come back here." Taking up the book, she said, "Thank you. Good bye."

I watched her walk out with the book in her hand. Then I turned to Mr. Skolnik. "Here's the money," I said, handing him the bill.

"You keep it. You made the sale. You earned it."

"But Mr. Skolnik, all I did was bring the book from the shelf. That isn't worth a dollar." He didn't answer. "Is it?"

"Oh, jah, I guess it is. Maybe you could work here, what you say?"

"Oh." This took me entirely by surprise. "I hadn't thought of that. Well, you know I'm not free all of the time. But I could come afternoons and Saturdays. You aren't open Sunday, are you?"

"No, no Sundays. Just regular days. Why don't you come work here? I think I use you to sell books."

It was an intriguing idea. I had discovered books by the time I was ten, so I was well on my way to becoming a lifetime reader. As a result of haunting the modest library of the Sisters of Mercy, I did know my way around books and book shelves. Then I had come across book reviews in the newspapers, too, which I had followed up by asking for the books at the city library.

"What hours you work, eh?" he asked.

"I could come about three in the afternoon on weekdays and stay until you close at seven. And I could work Saturdays all day, I think."

"Okay. Fours hours a day, five days—twenty hours. Eight to seven on Saturday, ten hours—thirty hours, jah?"

"Yes."

"How much?"

"How much what?"

"How much you pay?"

"You mean I have to pay you to work here?"

"Nah," he smiled. "I pay. You work. How much?"

"Oh. Well, I never thought of that. Thirty hours." I knew that some workers were getting paid fifty cents an hour, so quickly I did the figuring in my head. Thirty hours at forty cents an hour would be twelve dollars.

"What about ten dollars a week? How does that sound?"

"Ten dollars? Well, we take in that much? Don't know." He leaned back in his chair behind the counter. "Tell you what. You sell more than ten dollars a week, pay be ten dollars. Okay?"

That sounded quite fair to me, so I agreed. After clearing it with Sister Margarita, the sister in charge of Sisters of Mercy, I started.

At first there were very few customers. Occasionally someone would wander in off the sidewalk and browse the shelves to see what we had, but much of the time, it wasn't a real customer, just someone filling time, maybe hoping to find a job lying around in the streets somewhere. In 1936 very few people had extra cash and, even though the books were modestly priced with hardly anything over a dollar, we didn't sell much. How Mr. Skolnik managed to keep the store open, I don't know. Maybe he had everything already paid for. But it didn't seem to worry him. He sat behind the counter and read his Polish newspaper, willing to talk occasionally, but he wasn't garrulous by any means. He and his wife lived about the store, so on Saturdays he would leave me in charge while he went upstairs for his noon meal. Then she would invite me up to share in their meager offering.

Because the Sisters of Mercy had drilled all of us orphans in staying busy at all times, I was very uncomfortable at times. Even though I wasn't getting paid if I didn't make any sales, I still didn't like just standing around. So I started working. At first I dusted the books. This was a dirty job as the dust had settled in with a vengeance, and I had to stop regularly to clean my dust cloth. However, this didn't take more than a week or so. Then what could I do?

The floors weren't clean, so I decided to scrub them. When Mr. Skolnik saw what I was about, he tried to stop me. "What you do?"

"I'm scrubbing the floors. They're filthy." I was on my hands and knees, looking up at him.

"You not a maid. No scrub."

"They need scrubbing, Mr. Skolnik. When I get finished, you'll see a great improvement." He stood silently for a moment, as if undecided. Then gently shaking his head, he retreated to his chair behind the counter.

Scrubbing floors is not pleasant work. It's hard on the knees, and it's impossible to protect the hands, but it had to be done, so I did it. After I had finished, the floors did look good, almost new. The boards didn't exactly shine, but I knew they were cleaner than they had been in some time.

After I had surveyed my work, I realized I should have first washed the window which fronted onto the street. The window was so dirty that what little light that managed to come in was in variegated shafts, rays of sunlight which shone through the dirty patches.

Washing the window was much easier than scrubbing the floor. Mr. Skolnik had a short ladder for reaching to the tops of the shelves, and this served quite well. I washed the window, both inside and outside twice each. When I finished, it was possible to see out without having to find a clean patch, and the light shone in as it should have.

I was standing, looking out the window when Mr. Skolnik came to stand beside me. "Clean," he said. "Clean."

"It looks better, doesn't it?" I asked, probably searching for a compliment.

"Ach, jah, clean." Smiling, he retreated to his chair behind the counter.

We still weren't selling many books, so some weeks I didn't earn very much. Then I began to ask myself how could I increase business?

How could I get people to come into the store? We had a modest supply of posters and art supplies at Sisters of Mercy so, with Sister Margarita's permission, I made some posters to put in the window, and then I made a sandwich board which I could stand on the sidewalk advertising specific books.

Mr. Skolnik could take orders for new books, but he didn't do much business that way. Most of his sales were used books, books bought from estates or from other stores, perhaps going out of business. I knew that paperboys advertised their daily newspapers by finding a story to highlight, so I decided to do the same with books.

The first book I chose was *Walden* which I had just read. On the sandwich board I wrote, "Life in the wilderness. Read about one man's escape from civilization. *Walden* by Henry David Thoreau."

It wasn't catchy at all, but I did see people stopping to read the sign, and a few actually came in, asking to see the book. Since we had only two copies of *Walden*, I had to try to divert their attention to something else, for what could I say if we had sold both of them?

As time went on, it became much easier to sell the books, and I began to earn my ten dollars a week. Now I had spending money and could buy new clothing for myself, especially underwear and stockings which no one else had ever worn. What a luxury that was.

I don't know how long it took me to realize it, but eventually I began to see that Mr. Skolnik couldn't read English. Oh, he could make out letters and words, but to actually sit down and read one of the books we had was probably beyond him. Then I saw why he never recognized the titles of the books. When someone told him what was in a book, he remembered it that way. That was why he knew about the white whale and not *Moby Dick* and rafting on the Mississippi instead of *The Adventures of Huckleberry Finn*. Still it was a curious way to deal with books, I saw.

After I had been working at Books for Less for a few weeks, I realized that we needed something more to attract people. Since people still bought magazines and newspapers, even during the Depression, I thought if we had a corner devoted to those, we would have more customers. I asked at the corner drugstore, and was given the name of the news distributor for southern California. At first he was hesitant, as we couldn't promise many sales, but I was persistent, and eventually he brought in a display case with newspapers and magazines. He also had some signs that we put up in the window, and gradually as people began to realize they could buy their favorites from us, our business increased. There wasn't much mark-up on either newspapers or magazines, but occasionally one of the newsstand customers bought a book, so eventually it began to pay off. After I began preparing a pot of coffee in the morning, customers began to frequent the store more regularly, too. At first, we gave the coffee to everyone free, but then we started charging five cents a cup which wasn't exorbitant.

After I had been working for Mr. Skolnik for several months and was earning my ten dollars a week regularly, I decided it was time for me to leave the Sisters of Mercy. Sister Margarita didn't like to let any of the girls go if she didn't have a position or a family to go to. But I had checked with Mrs. Watson and determined I could live with her at her rooming house for five dollars a week, and that included meals. Then after I left the Sisters of Mercy, I could increase my hours at the bookstore.

Mr. Skolnik wasn't receptive to this at first. "How many hours a week?" he asked.

"Sixty. From eight to seven at night, every day except Sunday."

"Sixty. Sixty, eh? And you wanting more money, eh?"

I nodded.

"How much?"

At forty cents an hour, I should be paid twenty-four dollars a week. I was hesitant to ask for that much, but I knew I was worth it as since I had begun working there the store was now clean and inviting, and I thought we were attracting better customers than formerly. "How much?" he asked again.

I gripped my resolve and announced, "Twenty-four dollars."

"Twenty-four dollars? Twenty-four dollars. And you be here all the time."

"Yes, except for lunch."

"And you take care of customers all?"

"Yes."

"I think about it," he announced.

I breathed a sigh of relief. At least if he was thinking about it there was a chance. I imagine he discussed it with his wife Olga, but the next day, he said, "Okay."

"Okay, what?" I asked, not realizing what he was okay-ing about.

"Okay twenty-four dollars a week."

"Oh, thank you, Mr. Skolnik. Thank you very much."

After that Mr. Skolnik spent less and less time behind the counter reading his Polish newspaper. I'm certain he still read it, but now he did it in their apartment. I suppose Mrs. Skolnik had mixed feelings about him being there all day, but she never mentioned it to me. And after that I began to regard Books for Less almost as my own store. I was now effectively on my own, earning my own money and supporting myself. I told myself I had come a long way from being discovered in a basket as a foundling.

Chapter Fourteen

After I became accustomed to working at Books for Less, I realized that the shelving system Mr. Skolnik had been using wasn't functional. In fact, I couldn't discover that he was using any system at all. Books were shoved in any which way with no regard for their contents, and books by the same authors were sometimes aisles away. What melange of contents that provoked. Thus, I began to re-arrange the books. At first I tried alphabetizing the books by their titles. This was the easiest way if someone knew the title of the book she wanted. However, as I soon discovered, people sometimes didn't know the title. Maybe they knew only the author's name, and if I hadn't heard of the author, we couldn't locate the book.

After a few weeks, I decided to re-shelve the books based on the author's last name. This system also didn't work. Now I could locate anybody's book if I knew the author. I didn't always.

I spoke to the librarian at the city library who told me their books were shelved according to the Library of Congress System. However, another system which was used by small libraries was the Dewey Decimal System. I read about both of these, but they seemed too complicated for me.

Finally, I happened onto an approach that worked. I separated the books by subject matter, just as the Dewey Decimal System does, but I didn't actually catalogue the books or assign them numbers. Once I had the fiction separate from the science, for example, then I alphabetized by the author's last name. This was still slightly flawed, but if the person knew the book was about the West, for example, or the Civil War, we could quite easily discover the books by any specific author. Since the fiction section was the largest, I put it first in the store. Thus, people entering would find stories first. Then I put biographies, autobiographies, and histories. The areas that had the fewest books I put farthest away from the front door.

By the time I was finished, I had moved each book several times, and I knew pretty well what books we had and I usually could direct a customer where to find a specific book or find it myself. Not only that I began to take proprietary pride in the book store. I knew I didn't own the store or the books, but still I was in charge, and all the books answered to me. So in a way I was the owner.

After we began offering coffee, I persuaded Mr. Skolnik to allow me to set up a card table with chairs so people could play cards, dominoes, checkers, or chess. Many of these customers were only loafers who didn't buy books, but they did add to the atmosphere and make the store a desirable place for others to come. Some of them wanted to chew tobacco, and for that they needed spittoons, but I refused to have them spitting into spittoons and then having to clean the filthy things. I relented and let them spit so long as they carried their own cans. The smoking I tried to discourage, but so many men smoked in those days, that I had to accept the constant odor of smoke and the need to empty the overflowing ashtrays. Unfortunately, the smell of smoke and ashes permeated everything in the store including my clothes and all of the books. But no smoking areas were far in the future in those days.

Since many of the people used the book store as a place for socialization, I thought why not take advantage of that and heighten its value. So I constructed and hung a bulletin board on which people could post notes to each other or place hand-written ads for a room to rent or handyman work available. Soon, the book store began to function as an actual community center, and I was at the center of everything.

This was all after I began working full-time at the store and, as a result, people began to identify me with the store and with community events since I was always there except for when I took my lunch. I tried leaving Mr. Skolnik in charge while I was gone, but for many reasons this was quite unsatisfactory. Thus, I made a sign to hang in the window; "Closed for Lunch."

Being identified with the store was pleasant to me as I had had no personal identify heretofore except as a denizen of the Sisters of Mercy. I reviewed the bulletin board regularly, removing out-of-date announcements and screening some which might be inappropriate. What I was discovering was that it was satisfying and rewarding to be out on my own in the community, earning a living and paying my way.

Whenever Mr. Skolnik could, he went to various sales where he bought up boxes of used books. These he had delivered to the back room of the store where they sat until I found time to go through them, sorting, and eventually shelving them appropriately. Fortunately, he never offered to help me as I had become somewhat particular and even exacting as to where each book belonged. I was afraid that he would simply shove a book in anywhere he found space. That would never do.

Occasionally a book was so worn that it was hardly worth adding to our stock. When that was the case, I set it aside and when I had several set up a table out front offering the books free. No one would take them. Then one day a salesman told me that people are always skeptical about anything that is free. He said, "Charge a nickel or a dime, and then they'll sell."

Following his advice, I made a sign which said, "Books; five cents." Then people bought them. So even the books in the worst condition were being sold.

One big advantage of working in the bookstore is that Mr. Skolnik never begrudged me reading. Not that I read on the job. There was hardly time to keep the place neat and the books shelved orderly without sitting down and losing myself in somebody else's imagined (or real) adventure. But Mr. Skolnik permitted me to take any book home with me. The result was that I spent most of my free time at Mrs. Watson's reading.

Occasionally I helped Mrs. Watson or Jeannie with the clean-up after supper since there was always that chore. Since I didn't arrive home until about 7:15, they saved my meal for me as the other boarders ate at 6:30, and they were always finished by the time I arrived. Several of them would be sitting in the dining room/living room listening to various programs on the radio, while Mrs. Watson, Jeannie, and I worked in the kitchen.

In those days we used real cups, saucers, plates, and silverware. Today I know many places that offer food do it on paper or Styrofoam, and the utensils are made of plastic which are discarded after they're used. We always used real plates and silverware which had to be washed following every meal.

We didn't have a dishwasher as at the Sisters of Mercy and cafeterias later had, so we washed by hand. But it was a pleasant duty, standing at the sink and talking with the two of them, learning what the life of a woman was like in the latter part of the Great Depression, listening to their gossip, and actually deriving some satisfaction from being a part of a community which included me. I found I was growing into womanhood, and I was enjoying the transition.

After we had the dishes washed and everything was prepared for breakfast the next day, I retreated to my room to read. At first I was not very discriminating about the books I read. I do remember reading Sir Walter Scott and other writers who were said to be classic authors. It was rich sinful pleasure to lose myself in *Ivanhoe*, or *The Black Prince*. Soon, however, I wanted more substance. I began to cast about in my reading, looking for something more.

One afternoon as I tackled a box of books to be shelved, I came up with an anthology of British literature. I recognized many of the authors from the table of contents, and almost immediately saw this was a book I had to read. I set it aside to take with me.

That night I read *Beowulf*. It was hard to understand, but it was in translation, and I continued until I finished it. It was exciting to me to realize that these words, even though translated, were over a thousand years old, and that despite the time difference the people depicted were similar to me, that they had some of the same fears and hopes that I did.

Next in the book came Chaucer. Chaucer's name we had heard at the Sisters of Mercy, but the sisters hadn't let us read him since they objected to his writing. This, too, was in translation, and even though parts of it weren't clear, I saw why the sisters protested; Chaucer was down to earth and even what could be called dirty. But there was a sense of life in Chaucer which couldn't be counterfeited. Chaucer was real, authentically real, and I looked forward to the day when I might read him in the original.

After that it was impossible for me to stop reading in that anthology. When I came to Shakespeare, I was excited. We had read and talked about *Julius Caesar*, so I knew the language might be challenging, but many of the words had definitions supplied in the margin and, by stopping to check them, I could follow the speeches without much difficulty. The book had *Hamlet* and *Macbeth*, both of which I read. I'm certain I didn't understand them fully, but I enjoyed them and looked forward to the day when I might talk about them with someone else.

After Shakespeare came many other fine authors until I found a section devoted to Samuel Pepys's diary. This had only short bits from the diary, but they were so interesting that I wanted to read the whole thing. We didn't have a copy of Pepys's diary in the book store, so I checked one out from the city library. Then I discovered why the entries in the anthology were so short.

Pepys had been a womanizer. His entries were camouflaged in a code which he created, but even so it was possible even for me to determine what he had written. At first I was shocked as any student of the Sisters of Mercy might be, but then I was excited and intrigued. What would cause a man to act as he had and then to record his actions, unapologetically in his diary? I read in great gulps of print, reading and digesting, thinking as I read, and trying to connect what had happened almost three hundred years earlier to my life in the late 1930s.

The next great author in the anthology was Samuel Johnson. He was such a massive thinker that it was daunting to read his writing. But when I compared him to Shakespeare, I liked Shakespeare better. Actually, I liked Chaucer and Pepys better, too, maybe because they were so straightforward in their writing.

That anthology of British literature delivered me out of the twentieth century. Even when I got to the war poets -- Stephen Spender, Rupert Brooke, Rosenberg, Gurney, and others -- I read them avidly, savoring the beautiful words and re-experiencing with them the horror, anguish, and awe of men gassing or killing each other. They truly made war an awful and frightful experience.

I think after I had read and re-read that anthology that I never approached reading and writing the same way again. Here was a world of experience between covers, available to any thinking and feeling person. In a way reading all of these great authors—from Alfred the Great to John Keats to T. S. Eliot separated me from the twentieth century, reducing my definition to something much less than I might have thought before, reminding me that life mattered to everyone, not just to me. In a way I stood outside myself, watching and analyzing, like Keats in his letter to his brothers when he talked about negative capability, the ability to hold two opposing ideas simultaneously without having to resolve them; that sounds paradoxical, but I thought I understood.

Thanks to that anthology my world was expanded, and I began to see that there was more to living than the Sisters of Mercy had prepared me for.

Chapter Fifteen

After I received the telegram notifying me of Edward's death, I retreated into myself. I was hurt that he was gone; he was the only person I had ever loved, and I didn't think I could ever care for anyone else again as I had him. I knew he had loved me, too, so this eased the pain slightly, but there were times when I faced the truth of never seeing him and it almost crushed me. How could I go on without his letters to buoy me up, to give me a reason for living?

Then I received word that he had placed his insurance in my name; that is, I was his beneficiary. There was enough money to buy myself a house, but I didn't want to act too quickly. I asked myself, "What would Edward want me to do?" I thought he would want me to wait.

Many banks had failed during the early 30s, but after 1933 when President Roosevelt closed the banks and re-opened them, I thought there was no need to be concerned, so I opened a savings account. The money would keep until I knew just what to do with it. However, I had already decided I would buy a house.

At the bookstore, things went on about the same. Mr. Skolnik let me run things as I wanted to, rarely interfering. In fact, I got the idea that he liked not having to worry about anything. He checked the register occasionally and took out money to make bank deposits, but otherwise, the everyday decisions were left up to me. I suppose Mrs. Skolnik had something to say about all of this, too, but she never mentioned anything to me, so it appeared everything was working satisfactorily.

What happened is that the job at Books for Less became very

important to me. I never calculated it, and I never would have predicted it, but it happened that I looked forward to going to work every day, and on Sunday I found myself planning what changes I should make or where I should clean up, or how I might use the shelf space better. There quickly developed a routine of running the store that began to seem almost like second nature; I enjoyed it and looked forward to it.

The magazine distributor, Mr. Tomkins, came every Saturday to remove the out-of-date newspapers and magazines which hadn't been sold. Sometimes he took those with him, but more often he simply tore off the covers; this was so they couldn't be sold. When he left them behind, I got to read them.

One Saturday, he came in as usual about three o'clock. Since our store was one of the last on his route, he didn't have to hurry and he often sat and enjoyed a cup of coffee.

"Alex," he called. "Why don't you ever sit down to a cup of coffee? I've been coming in here for several weeks, but I've never seen you sit down."

"There is always work to be done, Mr. Tomkins."

"But the work will wait, won't it? It doesn't all have to be done today."

"No, I suppose not, but still I have to wait on customers and keep the shelves neat and not let the floor get too dirty—"

"Alex, the world isn't going to end tomorrow. How about you coming out with me to have supper some place?"

This was a new thought entirely. I had regarded Mr. Tomkins as a business associate only. While he was not so much older than I—not more than thirty, I guessed—and he was relatively attractive, there was something about him that I didn't like. For one thing he wasn't anything like Edward. I already knew that I was fated to be true to Edward's memory, and I didn't want to think I could be attracted away from that core of memory we two had defined.

One aspect of Mr. Tomkins that I was not attracted to was his dress. As all men did those days, he wore a hat, but he wore it in such a way that it looked as though he meant to challenge the world. He had it tilted to the side slightly, and lifted in front so it perched atop his head. He always wore a suit, but most of the time the backs of the knees were wrinkled from his sitting down, and there were food stains on the jacket. I suspected his shirt probably wasn't entirely clean either. Not only that but his fingernails were almost always dirty. Was it just ink? I didn't know.

"Well, what do you say?" He interrupted my thoughts.

"Oh, no, I couldn't do that."

"Why not? You're not married are you?"

"No, I'm not married."

"Do you have a beau? Are you promised?"

"Yes," I said slowly. "I am promised." Perhaps this was equivocation, but I felt I was promised to Edward's memory, and I wasn't going to let it go for supper with a traveling salesman or news distributor.

"And you couldn't even have supper with me? I could show you a good time, Alex. Say, what does that Alex stand for, anyway? That's not your real name, is it?"

"No. My name is Alexandria."

"Alexandria? Whew. That's some name. Come on, why not go with me to have supper?"

"Mr. Tomkins, I appreciate the offer, but I simply can't. Thank you for asking."

Evidently he recognized my resolve, or at least that's what I saw in his face. "Well, if you ever change your mind, just let me know. We could have a good time."

After that it seemed that whenever Mr. Tomkins came in, he spoke to me a bit more familiarly than he had before, but since I didn't respond any differently, I think he realized that I wasn't available to him. I don't think he ever gave up, fully, however. Maybe he was just tempting me, like the devil, seeing whether I could resist him. Since he didn't appeal to me, I could and did.

Chapter Sixteen

One of the greatest benefits of working at Books for Less is that I developed a much greater appreciation for books. Oh, I had loved reading long before I started working for Mr. Skolnik, but now I began to see the actual, physical book in a different light. One of the first points of awareness was the smell.

The smell of books is not universal. A book can carry almost all the smells of its owner without the owner being aware of it. If the owner smoked, the book will smell like smoke or ashes. Sometimes that can be overpowering. Other books smell like their owner's perfume, as if the owner actually sprayed the book or used it to press flower petals. A book could smell like pine needles or peppermint. Those books with the evocative smells are the ones that seemed to speak to my olfactory system the loudest.

Then books that have been stored in attics or cellars have a different smell: musty and moldy at times. If they are damp, they probably have to be dried before they should be shelved. The smell remains after drying, however, and if the mold or must is too strong, the book may have to be discarded. (Years later I learned that a sheet of Bounce fabric softener would remove the odor.) What I did with those books first was to consign them to the table out front where they sat in the sun and enjoyed the fresh air. Sometimes that was enough to redeem them. Then I could shelve them like any other.

Occasionally we got a book which was warped. Evidently it had been wetted and allowed to dry into a different shape, or it had been crushed somehow under furniture or other books. I always tried to reclaim those books, but I wasn't always successful. Sometimes the transformation of its shape appeared to be permanent; if so, I resigned a warped book to the bargain table.

Of course a new book has a different smell from a used one. Evidently the paper used contributes to the new book smell. Whatever it is, there is an odor which isn't always bad; sometimes it is even attractive. New books have their own identifiable aroma, and I grew to like the smell despite the fact that we had very few new books at Books for Less. Many of the old books were relatively neutral insofar as their smell, unlike the new ones.

The new books always excited me, I suppose the way new clothing did. To think that no one else had ever read these words before was like being the first to wear a dress or any other garment; there was something rich and indulgent about it. I always appreciated opening a shipment of new books, even though I knew they were usually ordered especially for a specific customer. I don't remember that I ever had a new book of my own in those days. However, I certainly didn't feel deprived. Just as I didn't mind wearing second-hand clothing, so, too, did I not mind reading a book which someone else had read before me. I could wear my books just as I wore my clothing.

Even the pages of the books excited me. I think I had never noticed before, but some pages are actually thinner than others. In some books the pages are so thin, one can almost see through them. They feel flimsy and delicate, like a butterfly's wings, but the print is there, and one can read them easily. Maybe the paper is thinner to allow the publisher more pages. I was always very careful with such pages, turning them extra carefully and never turning down the corner of a page.

One factor which could increase or decrease my pleasure in a book was underlining. Some of the textbooks, especially, had extensive underlining, as though the reader wasn't sure specifically what to underline, so he or she underlined nearly everything. This was a distraction to my eyes as, while I read the words, I was simultaneously trying to read the underlining. When the books' underlining was more restricted—to main ideas, for example—then I enjoyed stopping to look at the highlighted words or sentences, trying to guess the plane of thinking of the former reader. Many years—even decades—later when it became popular to highlight words or sentences rather than underline them, I thought the highlighting was an improvement. It didn't seem to interfere with the print as much as underlining did.

It was nearly always rewarding to find marginal notations in the books. These were an extension of the personality of the former owner, and I enjoyed speculating who that reader was; the marginal notes were like clues in a detective story which, if I could decipher them carefully, would give me a definition of that person.

One more factor in my appreciation of books was their size. They ranged all the way from tiny, child-sized books—almost booklets—to what today are referred to as coffee table books. These latter were always aggressive and seemed to want to take over their surroundings. They probably needed to be displayed by themselves as they were much larger than their peers. As a result of their outsized definition, I had to keep the large books on a separate shelf, usually stacked flat as I didn't want to waste space by raising the next shelf too far above. Some of these were reference books, like atlases, but others had extensive photographs and were meant to be savored visually rather than appreciated for their words. These out-sized books always struck me as a type of hybrid, not really deserving to be categorized along with regular books.

The touch of a book, the way it felt, seemed to be an extension of its size. A book that could be comfortably held in one hand provoked a different response in me than one which demanded that both hands come into play. This sense of touch is quite subtle, I realize, but sometimes the sense of touch eludes us in other matters, too. We say we are touched by something when in actually we mean we react emotionally. I guess much of my reaction to books is emotional.

The definition of book hasn't always been agreed upon. I recently discovered in my reading that UNSCO has defined a book as a "non-periodical printed publication of at least 49 pages excluding covers." This omits some books published for children as many of them do not have 49 pages. It also relegates pamphlets and brochures to another category.

I suppose I should define my relation to books as a love affair; it was facilitated by working at Books for Less. It wasn't so much that I had to own books or collect them as it was I just wanted to know what was in them. Since I didn't have to buy them or check them out from the library, I came to feel that I was in the best of all possible worlds.

In a way, books became my friends without whom I would have been lost. I lived among them by day and lived in them by night. For a time it seemed a perfect arrangement.

Chapter Seventeen

Suddenly, it seemed, we were in World War II. After the war which ended in 1918, most Americans felt that Europe should handle its own problems. If Europeans wanted to go to war, let them. But December 7th, 1941 changed all that. Now it became a personal matter for many people. After the bombing of Pearl Harbor, Americans were no longer isolationist. Even though the United States wasn't prepared for war, on December 8th President Roosevelt asked Congress for a resolution declaring war against the Empire of Japan. It was passed almost unanimously.

Some men hadn't waited and had already enlisted based on what they expected to happen in Europe. Others enlisted early on the morning of December 8th. Young men dropped out of college—some even left high school—to enlist.

Of course we had no idea what this would mean to us civilians. It became clearer when the Food Rationing Program was begun in the spring of 1942. Everyone would be required to make sacrifices. Rationing became a pattern of life which lasted for four years.

One positive benefit of the war was a rise in employment. It appeared that the Depression was at last ended with jobs for every able-bodied man. Women, too, began to work outside the home in greater numbers than ever before.

Everybody was encouraged to participate in scrap drives, collecting paper, rubber, aluminum—anything to aid the war effort. Grade school children collected tin foil and rolled it up into balls. Boy and Girl Scouts came around, asking for paper. Scrap iron drives were regularly held.

Mr. Skolnik got a poster which we put up in the front window of Books for Less. It announced "Save Your Cans: Help Pass the Ammunition." There was a soldier using what might have been a machine gun, but the ammunition was cans held out by the hand and arm of evidently a housewife. At the lower left of the poster was this: "Prepare Your Tin Cans for War: 1. Remove Tops and Bottoms; 2. Take off Paper Labels; 3. Wash Thoroughly, and 4. Flatten Firmly."

In 1943 sugar rationing began with the distribution of Sugar Buying Cards. Each family was asked to register. Coupons were distributed based on family size, and the coupon book allowed one to buy a specified amount. Of course, if there was no sugar available, the coupon did no good.

There were both Red and Blue stamp rationing. Red stamp rationing covered all meat, butter, fat, and oils, and most cheese. One result of the rationing was substituting what was available for what was not. Oleo, for example became the usual replacement for butter.

Blue stamp rationing covered canned, bottled, and frozen fruits and vegetables, juices and dry beans, and soups, baby food, and catsup. Each family was issued a War Ration Book which authorized purchase of rationed goods in the quantity and time named.

There was also a point system which was confusing to many people. Other products rationed were clothing, shoes, coffee, gasoline, tires, and fuel oil. If someone wanted to visit a friend in the country but had no gasoline for his automobile, he couldn't buy it unless he had gasoline stamps. The various salesmen that I talked to during those years complained about always having to worry about gasoline and not being free to buy tires when they needed them.

Out of rationing developed a black market where people could buy just about any rationed product without the stamps. Most Americans I knew frowned on this, however, as we were trying to support the United States' war effort, and rationing was the way to keep our boys safe overseas. I suppose all of us knew someone who knew someone else who could get whatever a person wanted, but I saw that as unpatriotic.

There was also a program of recycling which was instituted with the government's encouragement. People were urged to save everything, even bacon grease, to help the war effort. It was said it could be used to make glycerin for explosives.

One of the best results to come out of the national drive to support our boys and to conserve was Victory Gardens. People were encouraged to plant, cultivate, grow, and harvest their own vegetables in their own yards. This was something new for city people, but many people accepted it, and by the end of the war it was estimated that twenty million victory gardens were producing about forty percent of America's vegetables.

Mrs. Watson was skeptical about the notion of planting a victory garden at first. "I think I'll just wait and see," she told Jeannie and me. But it wasn't very many weeks later that she decided to cultivate her own victory garden in the back yard of her boarding house. She encouraged the boarders to help with the garden, and some of us did, with the result that by the end of the summer we harvested tomatoes, carrots, beets, corn, and green beans. The fresh vegetables were welcome additions to the meals, and what was left over Mrs. Watson and Jeannie put up for winter.

After a season or two the victory gardens were a standard part of everyone's life. People just took them for granted. As long as the war lasted, they would grow their own vegetables.

When the war ended, however, people realized that they were tired of rationing. They wanted to buy as much food as they wanted without having to bother with stamps. The changeover took several months, however, and it wasn't until 1946 that all the rationing stamps were used up.

People who wanted to buy a new automobile had to wait, too, since most of the manufacturing of the United States had been switched over to the war effort. I think it wasn't until 1947 that new cars were available for purchase again. By that time millions of servicemen and -women had come home, hoping to resume their lives and settle down to raise families.

Chapter Eighteen

Religion was not the same for me after I left the orphanage. It wasn't that I rejected it or anything like that—I didn't suddenly become an atheist—but after I got out on my own, I began to question its relevance in my life. Where did religion belong? I suppose part of this questioning was caused by the sisters' training. When we were required to imitate their selfless behavior, there was no need to think about it at all; all we did was follow orders.

At first, after I was liberated, I continued to go to church every Sunday. But one Sunday—I don't remember why—I just didn't want to spend that hour in church. Was this a form of rebellion? I suppose it was. We're supposed to keep holy the Sabbath the commandment says, and of course I felt guilty afterwards. It wasn't that I had anything special to do or that I felt any antagonism: I simply didn't want to go to church.

I believe my behavior was caused partially by the regimentation of the sisters of Mercy. When I got old enough to realize my own direction in life, then I had to try to define religion and make it relevant. This the sisters never did. In fact, if any of us asked questions that they might term impertinent, we were punished. Thus, we learned early on not to ask questions, impertinent or not. Since then I've learned that questions are the best way to learn anything, but I think the sisters either didn't want us to learn what they knew, or they were doubtful of the truth or worth of their position. Probably they were protecting their sense of investiture—their purpose was defined and I suppose they were jealous of it. Why should they share it with us, mere students, who didn't exhibit the respect and devotion which their position demanded?

For example, we were required to do religious retreats after we got to be six years old. Until then we lived in a world of innocence, protected from sin and damnation. Oh, we were punished for wrongdoing, but it was the sort of punishment that was non-thinking and almost non-committal, as if it didn't matter.

But after the sixth birthday everyone suffered together. The retreats were to be offered up to Jesus and Mary, to try to redeem our poor sinful selves in punishment and abasement of the body. My knees suffered the most, I think. Hours and hours of kneeling—and woe to anyone who slumped back against the pew—rapping on the skull was the penalty.

Sleep deprivation was next. I remember praying for sleep—and even going to sleep momentarily on my knees: anything to ease the burning of my eyes and the aching of my tired body. I used to think that I would never, ever willingly go on a retreat again.

Eventually I did come to value the retreats, but that was after I saw that I was committing myself; before that I was threatened by corporal punishment for being human. When I committed myself to a retreat of my own free will, then I could offer up myself and my pain. Prior to that it was little more than following of orders. Either that or suffer the consequences. Even afterwards, however, I think I never felt the sense of commitment which the sisters evidently enjoyed.

Another part of our religious existence at the Sisters of Mercy was prayer. It was required that we pray. My problem was there were times I could not pray. I knelt in physical posture, my body demonstrating subservience and obedience, but no words—no thoughts—manifested themselves. Then I was dry as a barren desert, no thoughts, no urges to connect—just emptiness. Why, I wondered, was I so empty when I did want to connect, to transcend, to realize something more than myself?

I had heard of the types of prayer and I knew them all, trying to include all of them when I prayed. Adoration, of course—to recognize God's greatness and glory and to pay homage. Contrition for my human state and for my weaknesses which at times appeared impossible to surmount. Thanksgiving for all the glories and wonders of this world and of His kingdom. Supplication I tried to save for special needs, to petition only for others—those in need—physically and emotionally.

I didn't consider myself important enough to ask anything for myself. If I could be instrumental in my small way in helping someone deal with life's trials, then so be it. But I could not, I would not pray for myself. Let God determine—I must simply obey, and I repeated, "Thy will be done." I suppose that, too, was a type of prayer.

This sense of questioning had been with me for years, beginning while I was still at the Sisters of Mercy. There was a time I could not partake of communion. I don't remember ever saying so to myself, but I think I felt that I was unworthy. I envied anyone who could participate in the miracle of transubstantiation, but I believe I felt it wasn't my lot in life—that it was only for others.

Finally Sister Charity spoke to me and asked me why I did not accept the host.

"Sister, I can't. I don't think I deserve it."

"You don't deserve it?"

"I'm filled with desires and urges which are un-Christian. I'm filled with sin."

"Do you believe in God?"

"Oh, yes."

"Then it isn't up to you to question God's beneficence, is it?"

"No, I suppose not."

"Don't you see that is what you're doing? Unless you accept God, you are setting yourself above Him. You must humble yourself before God."

Treated logically this way, it made sense. I was forced to accept God's grace and love; not to accept it was to place myself above Him. But that meant I couldn't think about it at all; all I could do was accept it. This made my brain itch. How could the sisters be so successful at subjugating themselves? Was it because they had no ego? At times this appeared to be true. They never seemed to do anything for themselves, always performing charitable acts for everyone else. Unfortunately, this made them seem less than human.

The matter of discipline they handled very effectively. Sister Margarita dispensed whatever punishment was to be meted out, and she did it apparently with no regard for the offender's feelings or regret of her own.

Why was discipline always so harsh and unforgiving, so unrelenting? Surely there were circumstances which ought to provoke some understanding, some amelioration of punishment? But no, discipline was discipline as unremitting as castor oil and just as unforgiving. The purgation of one's soul was not for the timid or the apologetic. Discipline was to be taken neat with no chaser.

Sister Charity, on the other hand, always understood. Why? I never could sort it out. How could anyone be so sympathetic and understanding at all times? Never blaming, never punishing, always understanding: it just didn't make sense. No one could be this perfect, not even Sister Charity. Still, she was highly preferable to Sister Margarita.

Today I attend a protestant church regularly. People are invited to partake of communion if they like, but no one is excluded as formerly was done at the Catholic services. The hymns are all sung in English with no Latin. Occasionally the choir will sing something in Latin— from a Mass, for example—but usually the hymns are the standard ones written by John or Charles Wesley and occasionally Martin Luther who was at one time a Catholic himself. When I first started attending this church, I didn't know any of the hymns or responses—I was still thinking in terms of "Kyrie Eleison" and "Tantum Ergo"—but eventually the hymns became familiar and I have come to regard them as old friends.

I have finally concluded that this matter of religion is too important to be left up to the Sisters of Mercy or to the clergy either. Each person must finally determine what she wants from religion. I suppose that speaks of a massive ego, but when it comes down to it, I do not want to be bossed around any longer as those sisters did the orphans. I want to think and choose for myself.

Chapter Nineteen

I could have continued to work at Books for Less for the rest of my life if nothing had changed. I liked the hours, I liked the responsibility, I was paid enough to live on, and Mr. Skolnik left me alone generally. Oh, we had to confer about special orders or re-ordering supplies, but as a rule he left everything up to me. As time went on, he let me decide more and more of the details of the store, and I began to regard it as my own. In a way this was good as it was teaching me independence, and I liked the sense of being my own person. In another way, perhaps, it wasn't so good as the time might come when I would be forced to give it all up, when I would have to look for another job or another path to independence.

It all ended one morning in November, 1943, when I opened the store to hear sounds of activity from the Skolnik's apartment above the store. Usually it was quiet above with only an occasional sound audible through the ceiling. In fact, it sounded like people running back and forth above my head, and I didn't believe either Mr. Skolnik or his wife could run.

After a few minutes, some men came down the stairs carrying someone on a stretcher. I saw they were ambulance personnel and they were carrying Mr. Skolnik. I watched in silence; Mrs. Skolnik trailed along behind the medical people, holding a handkerchief to her face. As she didn't appear to see me, I reached out to touch her arm and stop her.

"Mrs. Skolnik. What happened?"

She stopped and focused on me, but she didn't appear to actually see me. "George," she said. "George--."

"Yes?" George was Mr. Skolnik's name.

"He had an attack."

"A heart attack?"

"Yes, I think so." She followed the ambulance men outside. I had seen the ambulance parked out in front of the store when I came to work, but I had paid it no attention. Through the window I watched as the men opened the back doors and slid the stretcher with Mr. Skolnik on it into the back. After Mrs. Skolnik climbed in, they closed the doors and drove away.

For the rest of the day I fretted, worrying about Mr. Skolnik, hoping he would be okay but not knowing anything. Finally in the early afternoon, Mrs. Skolnik stumbled through the door. She looked exhausted. I ran to her to take her arm and help her into a chair. "Would you like some coffee, Olga?"

She nodded, so I brought her a cup and sat down beside her. "How is Mr. Skolnik?"

"Mr.Skolnik?" she repeated.

"Yes; how is he?"

"Oh, he's—he's--."

I waited, but she didn't go on. Reaching out to touch her arm, I asked again, "How is he? Is he all right?"

"No," she answered finally. "No, he isn't."

She sat quietly, holding the cup but not drinking. I hesitated to believe her, so I asked, "Do you mean he will have to stay in the hospital?"

"No, no hospital."

For some reason she didn't want to say anything more, but I wanted to know how Mr. Skolnik was. "Will he be coming home, then?"

She looked directly at me then before she said, "No. He won't be coming home." Her look of distress was so painful that I wanted to look away, to stop looking at her, but I couldn't. I saw tears begin at the corners of her eyes, but she didn't blink them away. "He won't be coming home."

"Then, he's--."

"Yes. He's gone."

There was nothing I could say. I felt my inadequacy as I saw Mrs. Skolnik needed comforting, but I was empty. She sat as still as an iceberg, holding the coffee but not drinking it. The tears began to seep out of her eyes, and I was touched by such a feeling of anguish that I almost began to cry myself. What would she do without Mr. Skolnik? What would become of Books for Less? What would I do? Would the store be closed up? If so I would have to find something else.

I ran to my purse and took out a handkerchief to give to Mrs. Skolnik. "Here," I said. "Try to drink your coffee."

She looked up at me as if she didn't recognize me. "He's gone," she said forlornly. "He's gone, and we didn't even get to say good bye. Thirty-seven years we were married. Thirty-seven years, and now it's over."

I reached over to raise her coffee up to her lips. When she felt the cup against her lip, she looked at it momentarily, evidently not recognizing it, but then she took a sip. A customer came in at that moment, so I had to leave her momentarily. When I returned, I saw she had been drinking her coffee and evidently she had wiped her eyes as her tears were gone.

"What will you do now, Olga?" I asked.

"Well now, that I don't know. George took care of everything, you know. He didn't want to bother me. But now, George is gone. Maybe--."

"Yes?"

"Maybe I should call the church. You know, Father O'Malley probably will know what to do."

"Yes. I'll call him for you."

I called the church and spoke to the receptionist who said that Father O'Malley would come over as soon as he could.

When I got back to Mrs. Skolnik, she sat in the chair, hardly moving and almost unaware. After I told her that Father O'Malley would be coming, she said, "That's good. He will know what to do."

"Should you lie down now to rest, Olga?" I asked.

"Rest? Why do I need to rest?"

"Well, I thought after all this, you might need to lie down."

"Oh. Yes. All right. I guess that would be good." She stood up, holding out the coffee cup which I took and then walked slowly back to the stairs and up to the apartment.

About a half hour later Father O'Malley from St. Agnes came. I watched him go up the stairs, relieved that it was his duty, not mine, to deal with such trauma.

When Father O'Malley came down the stairs, he stopped to talk to me. "You're Alexandria, aren't you?" he asked.

"Yes, Father. I run the store here for Mr. Skolnik. And Mrs. Skolnik, too."

"Well, I don't know about that. I don't think Mrs. Skolnik is going to be in any frame of mind to talk business any time soon. I will arrange for the funeral for George, but after that, I guess we'll just have to see."

The funeral was held on Saturday morning at St. Agnes Church. I closed the shop and put a sign in the window in case anybody should want a book. There were only a few mourners and no one from an immediate family except Mrs. Skolnik. I didn't remember that the Skolniks had any children, and I knew most of their relatives lived either in New York or Poland. The rest of the mourners were members of St. Agnes, evidently, who probably attended every funeral.

After the service, the altar guild served refreshments in the parish hall, so I went to pay my respects.

"Olga, what do you think you will do?" I asked.

"Oh, I don't know. I think I have to get somebody to tell me. Maybe Father O'Malley can recommend someone."

A few days later one of the businessmen who was a member of St. Agnes came to see Mrs. Skolnik and, after they talked for about an hour, he told me that she had decided to sell the store and move back to New York. I had expected this, so it was no surprise, but even so it was distressing. I didn't look forward to such a major change in my life, especially when I loved looking after the books and managing the store. What could I do now?

I had told Mrs. Watson and Jeannie both about Mrs. Skolnik's death, so they, too, suspected change was coming. That night while we washed the dishes, I asked them if they had any idea what I might do.

"Well, I'm afraid I can't use you here," Mrs. Watson said. "I mean, you're a good worker and all, but I don't think I could pay you enough."

"Oh, no, I wouldn't think of even asking--."

"But what I can do is let you stay until you find something. You know, until you get your feet on the ground. Maybe later when you get another job and are earning money, you can pay me."

I hugged Mrs. Watson and tried to wipe my eyes without her seeing.

Jeannie asked, "What else can you do, Alex? What other work have you done?"

"Well, that's just the problem. I've never worked at anything else. I don't have any skills besides working in that book store."

"But, Alex," Mrs. Watson said. "You've handled inventory, you've made change, you know how to wait on customers. Surely those are skills that you could use."

"I guess so."

"You know," Jeannie said. "I've been thinking. You grew up with a bunch of other girls, didn't you?" I nodded. "So you know how to take care of children. Right?"

"Yes."

"All right. With so many men in the service and so many women going to work, the mothers need someone to take care of their children; you know, professional baby-sitting. Maybe that's what you should consider."

Mrs. Watson beamed. "I think that might be it. Alex, what do you think?"

At first I was skeptical, but I nodded since I had come up with nothing on my own. "Maybe so. How would I start?"

"Well," Jeannie said, "there's a baby-sitting center just two blocks over. Why don't you go there and apply? All they can do is say no."

Suddenly I was afraid of even trying. No one wants to fail, but at that moment, I thought that even asking about a job would be presumptuous. "But with no experience--."

"What do you mean, 'no experience'? You've got all that experience at the Sisters of Mercy."

So it was decided among the three of us that I would apply at the Children's Care Center.

At it turned out, my fears were groundless. I met the owner/manager, Mrs. Lewis, and immediately felt at home in the Center. Children of all ages up to school age and even one or two in grade school were running around playing outside or sitting at a table inside coloring or painting. There were several babies sleeping or just resting in cribs, and the whole atmosphere was trusting and satisfying. I thought I would enjoy working there and, as it turned out, I wasn't wrong. In fact, the change was quite positive.

Chapter Twenty

I never spoke to Olga about how she should dispose of Books for Less, but I learned from the flyer which was posted in the window that there was to be an auction. I wondered about this since we hadn't been selling all that many books anyway; how much would books bring at an auction? Then the flyer was taken down and Father O'Malley told me that she had decided not to have an auction; she was selling everything as it was. Later I learned that she had accepted an offer which sounded quite reasonable; it wasn't extravagant, but it wasn't too small either. At the time I regretted not bidding on the store myself. I had enjoyed my time there, and I loved the books. But still, I didn't want to use the money in the bank from the U.S. Navy to buy a book store and the books which really weren't very profitable. We had been selling barely enough to pay my wages. So I watched as the bookstore changed hands, and I saw little changes put into effect. Mrs. Skolnik didn't stay around; as soon as the sale was final, she left for New York.

My job at the Children's Care Center wasn't overly challenging. I was to be there by seven as many of the women who worked for the munitions plants and so on started at eight, and I stayed until six; most of the children were picked up at five or just after. At first it was hectic as mothers came in with their children, left them with a hurried hug or kiss and were gone. Immediately the responsibility for the children was transferred to us. I watched Emma and Sharon DuBois, the assistant manager, and quickly saw what to do. The children had to be checked in, their possessions noted, and given something to do. It was not good to allow them to cry for their mothers. Actually, the checking-in was the easy part. What took me some time was learning how to deal with each individual child.

In the mornings there was always some child who didn't want to be left, who protested vocally about his or her mother leaving, and that child had to be comforted. By watching Emma and Sharon, I learned that the best approach was simply to comfort the child momentarily and then have him or her move on to something else. I gave them pictures to color, blocks to stack, or some other diversion so that they forgot within a few moments that they were sad.

Emma always had treats for the children at mid-morning and mid-afternoon besides lunch at noon. As I watched her and learned how to be a caregiver myself, I saw that Emma was devoted to the children. Running the care center was certainly more than just a job to her. Sharon, too, demonstrated a level of caring which was positive and impressive. Thus, with them as models, I believe I became someone for the children to look forward to. At least some of them did.

A few were taken by my name and took some sort of joy in calling me Alex. I didn't mind this, as Alexandria was a mouthful for small children. Some of them knew that Alex was usually a boy's name, so they questioned me, but it was merely inquisitive, not anything else. In a short time I began to see that they regarded me differently from Emma and Sharon; I don't know how it happened, but there were times when they wanted only me. This occurred in moments of stress—a skinned knee or elbow, or some trauma at home that they were having to deal with. Then they came to me, and I eagerly received them in my arms. In fact, one of the overriding joys of the job was that I got so many hugs over the course of a day. I remembered back to the Sisters of Mercy when there had been hardly any physical contact at all. One might have thought that the sisters and the orphans had no feelings whatsoever.

With the children at the care center, however, they embraced their feelings and they were ready to demonstrate them, whether in anger or joy. The anger we curtailed as best we could, admitting to ourselves that there were times when children deserved to be angry; at other times the anger was only incidental as when someone took a toy or interfered with play somehow. We soothed them as best we could at those moments, dried their tears which usually didn't last long anyway, and gladly shared their joys.

Occasionally a mother would bring treats for everyone in order to celebrate her child's birthday. Those were special days, especially if there was an actual birthday cake. This was rare, of course, as making cakes during the days of rationing required not only skill but also ingenuity—the ingredients simply weren't available.

These celebrations reminded me of the days we had enjoyed at the Sisters of Mercy for the special holidays: a break from routine which reminded us all that it was good to be alive and to have something to look forward to. However, the parties, if such they were, were not extravagant. In my older years I have learned that parents have become totally extravagant in celebrating the birthdays of their offspring, booking pizza parlors, gymnasiums, or dance studios, all in addition to the obligatory gifts for everyone, cake, and punch.

Our children were generally well behaved, and they enjoyed the parties, modest though they were. Very quickly I learned to love them and to enjoy my work at the center. In fact, it happened so gradually that I was hardly aware of it, but soon I saw that I no longer missed working at Books for Less. When this thought occurred to me, I felt a sense of disloyalty, as if I had betrayed a friend or a cause.

I still loved to read and spent many evenings at Mrs. Watson's reading, but now I didn't have to care about the individual books to the same extent as I formerly had. Now I could put the book aside when I had finished reading it for the evening or when I returned it to the library, and there was no ongoing concern. I think the children had displaced books for me. This wasn't an easy conclusion for me to reach, but when I analyzed it from several different angles, I saw it was true: I no longer needed books as I had. The children had become my life.

Chapter Twenty-One

On a beautiful spring day, I became aware that the children were somewhat over-active. I had grown accustomed to the way they acted and their behavior generally conformed to the weather. If it was a cold, rainy day, we caretakers knew we had our hands full. For some reason the children behaved differently when they were forced to stay inside. But on a sunshiny day that let them play outside, we expected them to be more settled and sedate even though more active. Their difficulties could be resolved easier.

Such was not so on this April day. Even though the sun was shining and the temperature was mild so they could play outside without coats, something was in the air. When I asked Emma about it, she said, "Oh, don't concern yourself. They'll get over it." But she said this with such an enigmatic smile that I wondered if something else were happening, something I hadn't been told about.

One of the babies had been fussy all day, and I had been charged with tending her. I had tried laying her down in a crib, but as soon as I put her down, she started squalling again, so I finally resigned myself to carrying her. Actually, I didn't mind holding a baby, since there was so much comfort from holding another person, even an incompletely formed one such as this who was about six months old. The only disadvantage is that it occupied one arm and hand so that I had to do everything with only half of my ability.

After lunch was over, we cleaned up the area and wiped the faces of those that needed attention. Then Emma announced, "All right, everyone. I have an announcement. Today we're celebrating a very special day, somebody's birthday!"

All the children had suspected this already, evidently, and that was why they had been so aggressive in their behavior. They had sensed something.

I shifted the baby from one arm to the other as I listened.

"This is a very special person to all of us, and I know you will all be glad to celebrate with us."

"Who is it?" one of the kindergarten girls asked.

"Someone whom you all know and love." She waited as the children looked around, wondering. I, too, was curious, as usually when we had birthday parties they were treated more sedately. Oh, we did sing and celebrate, but generally it was with less ceremony.

"Tell us, tell us," the children cried.

"Today we're celebrating the birthday of—Alexandria Hodgeman!"

The children raised their voices in cheers and hoorays. I'm sure I was something to wonder at as I stood there holding the baby.

"Alex, come to the front of the room," Emma called to me. I looked around, in a bit of a daze, actually, quite unsure of what was happening or what I was to do. "Alex," Emma called. "Come up here."

Slowly I walked to the front of the room where Emma waited. She beamed at me in pleasure. I had been caught totally unaware. Never before had I been the recipient of a birthday party. In fact, we never had birthday parties at the Sisters of Mercy. Birthdays were just one of three hundred and sixty-five days in the year, not marked by ceremony or even recognition. If we happened to know it was someone's birthday, we might fashion a birthday card for her during art period, but that and small gifts was all. There was no cake, no singing, no special recognition.

When I reached Emma, she said, "Here, let me take baby Emmaline."

"No," I answered. "I'll hold her. I want to." For some reason I needed the reassurance of a human body and, even though Emmaline was just a baby, she provided some recognition in me that a connection was important.

"Here," Emma said, taking my arm. "Turn around to face the

children." I allowed her to steer me about. "Now, children, I want you all to join in singing 'Happy Birthday' for Alex as today—April 23rd—is her birthday."

As the children, Emma, and Sharon sang, I began to cry. I think I was smiling through my tears, and I wanted not to cry, but I was touched, and maybe tears was the proper response. After they finished, Emma turned to me again. "Today *is* your birthday, isn't it?" she asked. I nodded as I remembered that on the application form I had completed I had had to put down a birthday.

"Well, Sharon and I have a small gift for you," Emma said as she held it out to me.

I took the wrapped gift in my free hand, not knowing what to do with it.

"Open it," the children cried.

"Yes, Alex, you should open it," Emma agreed.

I tried to grapple with the paper, but with one hand, it was impossible. "Here," Emma said. "Let me hold Emmaline." I hesitated. "For just a moment; while you open your gift."

Reluctantly I handed Emmaline to Emma. Never having received a gift in such a way and never being the center of attention like this, I really didn't know how to behave. I had seen birthdays for the children, but they were so unselfconscious that nothing appeared to faze them.

There was a small box inside the wrapping paper. Inside was a silver cross on a chain. I held it up for everyone to see. It shone and reflected light. "There's writing on the back," Emma said, so I turned it over. "Why don't you read it aloud? Quiet please, children, while Alex reads what the cross says."

I wiped the tears out of my eyes and read the inscription: "To Alex, 4-23-44, Children's Care Center, with love."

"We wanted to have 'Alexandria' put on it, but there wasn't room." I saw that the print did take up all of the space. "Do you like it?"

"Oh, yes," I answered. "I love it." I held it up for the children to see, and then I bent down so each one could come to look at it and to admire it. The last one was Ernest, a chubby two-year-old that everybody loved. He made his way up to where I was kneeling, stopped to hold the cross and, then, surprisingly, he bent forward to kiss it. What caused him to do this? What was it that elicited this immense act at that moment? I have worried at this for decades, and I still do not know.

Such an act of grace filled me with awe and I froze right there. Then I stood up, reclaimed baby Emmaline, and listened as Emma continued.

"Now, children, we have a special treat for today. Of course we have cake and ice cream to celebrate with."

The children voiced their approval at this. "But first, we're going to have our photograph taken. I've hired a photographer to take everyone's picture."

Sharon escorted a man carrying a camera into the room. "Now, all of you have to arrange yourselves in rows up here. Children in front may sit on the floor."

Soon the children had gathered in a semblance of order. With Emma standing to my right and Sharon on my left, we stood behind the children. Emma hung the chain about my neck and positioned the cross so it was visible outside my dress. Then the photographer called us all to attention. When everyone was situated, he reminded us not to move; then there was a flash, and it was done. For insurance he took another photo, but this was anticlimactic.

Following the photograph, Sharon brought out the cake and ice cream and the children lined up with the usual jostling and jockeying for position, but all in good spirits.

I stood silently, holding baby Emmaline, being reassured by her, wondering at the way the world turns, how this had all come about, and how it had occurred to me. I didn't think I deserved such attention and recognition, but it had happened, and it was up to me to deal with it positively.

When Sharon brought me a small piece of cake with some ice cream beside it, I took it and sat down at one of the children's tables, still holding Emmaline. "Happy birthday, Alex," Sharon said.

"Thank you, Sharon." I must have eaten the cake and ice cream as when I came to myself, it was all gone and there was a slight smear of ice cream on Emmaline's lips. Using a napkin, I wiped it off and tried to collect myself.

As I considered what had happened, what had been given to me, it occurred to me that there was a greater sense of love and mercy here at the Children's Center than I had ever witnessed at the Sisters of Mercy. The Sisters of Mercy nuns hadn't been insensitive, merely brusque and businesslike, but beyond that I never got the feeling that what they did was motivated by love or consideration. At times they seemed merely to be going through the motions, like one of Capek's robots in his play *RUR*. But today, I knew, I had witnessed, had actually been the recipient of, God's true love and caring.

Later, when Emma presented me with the photograph from that day, I was again stunned into silence, remembering and savoring what had taken place. The very day itself seemed to be burnished into my memory like acid etched onto a plate, leaving an indentation or recollection that would never be effaced. In the photo the children were all looking up eagerly into the camera, not knowing they were actually looking into the future; Emma and Sharon were quietly attentive and facing the camera with dignity; I, with baby Emmaline cradled in my arm, stood with a dazed look on my face, uncertain of myself and not totally aware of what was transpiring.

Today I have that photograph yet. Sixty-six years old it is and slightly faded, but everyone is still there, hungrily offering themselves to the camera lens, not anticipating their future selves, not fearing the future at all, just satisfied—even happy—to have their picture taken. The cross I have kept also, and occasionally I turn it over to read the tiny inscription on the back, treasuring it and valuing it beyond its monetary cost. It is slightly tarnished, but that certainly doesn't denigrate its value for me. But the photo comes closer to capturing the day and the memory. With baby Emmaline, I stand and face the camera, somewhat unsure, yet with an air of defiance: "I can deal with whatever the world gives me," I seem to be saying in that pose. The baby lies against my breast, content and almost asleep, the picture of happiness and comfort.

Chapter Twenty-Two

It took hardly any time after I began working at the children's care center before I saw that this was to be my life's work. I had enjoyed working at Books for Less, but now I discovered a richer, fuller meaning. Now I was no longer serving only myself as I had been; now I was extending myself to others, to children. I found I had to be serving others. When I simply worked—not helping anyone—I was destitute of feeling, of commitment, of purpose. I often lay awake at night, wondering why I even existed. Life was empty of purpose.

It was only through helping others that I began to see what the purpose of my existence was. "Man does not live by bread alone," Jesus said, and I could not live for myself alone. Only then did the true meaning of existence illuminate me and permit my light to shine. Only then did I accept my being had a reason, a rationale. Then did I truly live.

Some of my feeling could be called happiness. I don't know that I could define true happiness except that for me it meant being content with what I was doing. I've been happy, never doubt that. I've looked up at the sky, seen the birds, the grass, and the trees, and I was contented. Only later did I see that was happiness.

When I consider happiness now, I see it as of a moment, rarely long in lasting. It's impossible to capture a moment anyway. But those moments shine forth in my memory like some newly-created star in heaven, eager to shine and share its light.

The greatest happiness, I think, came when I was holding children. It's not up to me to say why—I can't anyway. But I knew the greatest joy when I held those babies and toddlers who needed me. Their need was pure—undiluted—and I fulfilled that need. I mattered and I was necessary. That joy seemed most intense when they were distressed—never mind over what—but even if it was just a hug for comfort it had so much value for me that nothing could compete with it. When I was holding a child, I was as much comforted as the child. This was heaven to me.

It took me a long time to understand my need for others. When I had been at the Sisters of Mercy, I had been taught to depend only on the sisters or on God. The implication was that other people would disappoint me, would let me down, and that I shouldn't trust them. But there were numerous times when I hungered for connection. I wanted one of the children to fall and scrape a knee or an elbow so I could offer comfort—yet receive it at the same time. Offering was only my way of getting love in return. For holding a child, stroking a brow, blotting a tear, or wiping a nose were only gestures toward connection. The children gave it willingly when they were stressed. Of course they didn't when they were playing or being busy. Then they did not wish to be bothered. But give them a little pain and their love was revealed, and I was the lucky recipient.

Of course, this didn't always work in my favor. Some of the children were easier to love than others, and these I began to see as my very own. Then I became jealous.

I was jealous all right. Bone-deep, marrow-rich throughout all of my poor existence I was jealous. Who the hell were these cursed mothers who came for children and took them away from me—bereft—the children crying and occasionally earning a back-handed cuff of correction—who were they? They had day jobs and husbands and children I would gladly have died for. Did they appreciate all this? Did they even see it? Not hardly.

I tried to contain my jealousy, but it burned through me at times like too much acid in the stomach, leaving me alone, sour, and hateful. But then a new day would come, the children would run into my eager, receptive arms, despite the resentment and spiteful looks of their mothers, and I was re-born to purpose all over again. Thank God the jealousy didn't last.

Even when I lost children—to family moves, to growing up—there seemed always to be more to take their place. It was a positive and redemptive existence God had granted me for which I gave thanks every night and at times during the day when everything seemed too perfect to continue. But it always did. It always did.

There were days when nothing seemed to go right, when the weather was nasty with rain coming down and the wind blowing, and the children had to stay inside, not liking it of course, and everyone seemed to be crosswise with the world. But even then, despite the runny noses and bathroom accidents, I think I saw what I had, and I believe I appreciated it.

In addition, once in a while a gift came my way. One of the deepest, richest, most touching, most profound experiences is to have a baby or toddler go to sleep in your arms. The first time this happened to me I was struck dumb with awe. It wasn't anything I had done, or was it? How could such deep-seated heartfelt pleasure come from such a little act? Who cares? Whose world has been changed? But I've been there and I've felt it, and I know no other physical pleasure to touch it. No other experience can even begin to shadow the profound depth of this one little happenstance. The curious part of it is one can't prepare for it. I've tried and failed. But suddenly the universe shifts, the baby or toddler comes to the haven of one's arms, and all creation relaxes. All strife, all tension, all stress are gone—banished to another waking time. For now sleep, deep peaceful, relaxing sleep comes to one; resting in the arms of Morpheus, the child succumbs to trust and comfort. This, this is what caused me to be born anew. Such trust and peace ought not to be so scarce.

Naturally I wasn't always a model of decorum. In fact, I developed negative feelings toward some of the mothers. There were some who didn't fully appreciate their children. I could see that in the way they left them in the morning, almost as if they were glad to be rid of them and in the evening when they came to pick them up, carrying their resentment like a sack of coal slung over their back.

I have never understood how a woman who had given birth to a child could ever say good-bye to that child. Of course, I've witnessed the trauma of their leaving their children for one day, and that can be truly distressing, but oftentimes it seems they just took it for granted. The children did, too. They got used to saying good-bye. I think I never could. To say good-bye even for a short while would traumatize me, I'm afraid.

Then I think of what would happen after the child grew up and left. Wouldn't saying good-bye be like cutting out part of your heart? I heard somebody quote Shakespeare once as saying, "Parting is such sweet sorrow." Talk about contradiction! How could it be sweet? Never for me. I think having children would be just taking a short cut to a broken heart.

Still, it wasn't always joyful and affirmative. There were days when I actually resented the babies who needed to be changed, the bottles that had to be heated, and the noses that needed to be wiped. Those days were hell. I'm not certain I believe in hell, despite what the Sisters of Mercy taught us, but I think for me hell would be having to do work with no satisfaction. Work with no real pleasure in it must be almost unendurable.

I have to be honest with myself when I admit that I have struck children. Actually it was only one child. But that once was sufficient for all of my lifetime.

The day was dark and long, filled with whiny, sick children, pulling at me, unraveling the sleeves of my personality, leaving me nothing but the thread of basic ego. I tried—I tried mightily—but everything just accelerated away from me and there was I running and stumbling, trying to catch up, trying to hold onto myself, all to no use.

Suddenly it was simply too much, more than a woman could bear. I struck out, struck a toddler, reaching to me for comfort and finding punishment instead.

It all ended. Everything froze. Her eyes looked at me in wonder—not accusation—how can this be? How could you strike me? And I, too, was stopped. All the noise, all the turmoil, the eddying of personalities and noise and strife just ended. Then I erupted. No volcano ever released a greater force than I did when I saw what I had done. Guilt, remorse, chagrin washed over me as a bath from Satan, letting me know how sinful I was. Opening my arms, I took her in and she—trusting ,never doubting—came to me through the grace of God. Oh how special and redemptive are the ways of God.

Chapter Twenty-Three

One evening as we were washing dishes, Jeannie asked, "Alex, what would you do if you didn't have to work?"

I stopped with my hands in the soapy water. "I don't understand. What do you mean?"

"What would you do with yourself if you never had to work? Suppose you had enough money to live on without working. What would you do?"

I shook my head and went back to washing. "I have no idea."

"Well, isn't there something you would like to do that working keeps you from doing? Don't you have any dreams? Any unrealized goals?"

"I guess I never thought about it. I've worked ever since I can remember. Even at the Sisters of Mercy--."

"But that's just what I mean. Suppose you didn't have to work? What would you do?"

I looked over at Mrs. Watson. "Don't ask me for help," she said. "I've worked all my life, too."

Jeannie shook her head in exasperation. "But don't you see? Work ties you down. Well, doesn't it? It keeps you from doing what you really want to do. What would you do if you never had to work again?"

I tried to think about this, but it was such a foreign concept to my very existence that I could see no way out of it. "I don't know," I answered. "I really don't. I've never thought about it."

"Well, think about it!" Jeannie said. "Wouldn't you like to travel? Maybe see the world? Boy, I would. I can just imagine what it would be like to travel to Europe, or Asia, or Africa. Think how adventurous that would be."

"I don't think it would be adventurous for me," Mrs. Watson said. "Probably the beds would be hard, or the temperatures would be too hot or cold, and think about the insects. I've read that in some places they have mosquitoes--."

"Mrs. Watson, you're missing the point," Jeannie interrupted. "The thing to do is to experience the world, to have adventures. You don't want to be stuck here running a boarding house all your life, do you?"

Mrs. Watson looked up from her cup of tea. "Jeannie, I think you don't realize who you're talking to."

"Oh, I know you've been here for years and it's what you're used to. But don't you ever wonder what it would be like to travel? To see what's out there?"

"No, I don't," Mrs. Watson said. "In fact, I think I would be very uncomfortable. The last time I rode a train for any distance it was extremely unpleasant. People crowded in with their kids crying. The seats were hard. And the smells. Well, I guess I'd just rather stay right here."

"But, but--. What about you, Alex? Don't you want to get out of southern California and experience more? You know there's more to life than working in a children's care center and reading books." When I didn't answer right away, she asked, "Well, don't you?"

"Maybe I don't, Jeannie. Maybe working at a children's care center, and washing dishes after dinner, and reading books is all I need."

"But, Alex, you can't just settle for things this way. Don't you see it?" She was almost pleading.

"What would you, do, Jeannie?" I asked.

"Oh, I know what I'd do all right. I'd buy all new clothes and catch the first train or boat out of here. Europe here I come. And I wouldn't stop there, either. I'd go right on to Asia and Africa. You name it, and I'd go there. I'd wear exotic clothes and eat foods the names of I couldn't even pronounce. And I'd drink drinks I've never even heard of before. I wouldn't stop until I had seen everything from Australia to the North Pole. God, how I would love to travel!"

As I drained the water from the sink, I looked over at Mrs. Watson who was smiling. "Don't you like it here, Jeannie?" she asked.

"Oh, sure, it's fine. It's just that I get tired of the same old routine every day. Working as a sales girl isn't very exciting, you know. I want more out of life than a new pair of sensible shoes every year."

"Maybe that's where we differ," I said as I wiped my hands. "In fact, I like what I do every day. I enjoy going to work."

"Well, I don't. If I had my way, I'd never work another day as long as I live."

Jeannie and I sat down at the kitchen table and poured ourselves tea.

"Well, Jeannie," Mrs. Watson said, "I don't see how you're ever going to make it happen."

"Not unless you marry somebody with a lot of money," I added.

"Well, don't think I wouldn't either," Jeannie asserted. "I'd give just about anything to get out of here and see what else the world has to offer. Haven't you heard the train whistles? In the night? Aren't they romantic? Don't they make you want to get on the next train and just ride to the end of the line? And then keep going?"

Of course I had heard the train whistles. I had to agree with Jeannie that they did sound romantic. They spoke of far-off places which I probably would never see where people dressed differently, ate unusual foods, and lived in ways that I couldn't even conceive of. Late at night as I was reading or even more so after I had turned off the light beside my bed, when I heard a train whistle, I wondered where the train was going, and whether I might ever get to go somewhere romantic, too.

One night as I was walking home after church I happened to see a train as it rushed past with the windows all lit up and people sitting behind the glass, reading or smoking. One car was a dining car, and I saw people eating a meal. I wondered what their lives were like, where they were going, and what they would be doing after they got there. What had they been doing so far that led them to be on the train at that moment? But then the train was past, and the moment, too, was gone. Like Keats, I could travel farther in my books than I ever could on a train or a bus. After the war, airplane travel became much more practical, but I didn't think travel by flying in a plane could ever measure up to the "realms of gold" that Keats referred to.

"Well, Jeannie, it's pleasant to consider, I guess, but I don't think any knight in shining armor will be coming on a white charger to save me from my life anytime soon. It looks as though I'm doomed." I tried to say this with a smile so she would know that I didn't feel doomed at all.

"Well, maybe you are," she agreed, ignoring my smile. "Maybe you'll be stuck here forever. Just like--."

"Careful what you say, Jeannie," Mrs. Watson said. "I don't mind being stuck here as you say."

"Oh, I'm sorry, but I just feel so trapped at times. I'm getting older, and what do I have to show for myself or to look forward to?"

We sat there at the kitchen table, letting the thought die of its own accord.

"Well," Mrs. Watson said as she stood up. "This isn't getting the table laid for breakfast."

I stood up, too. "I'll help," I said.

Jeannie stayed sitting at the table, gazing off somewhere in the distance, lost in her thoughts and evidently wishing for a different existence. I couldn't speak for Mrs. Watson, but as for me I was relatively content. I didn't feel the need for a man in my life as I knew there was no one who could ever measure up to what I had enjoyed with Edward. My work was satisfying, too. I just hoped that Jeannie might some day come to accept her life instead of wishing for something else. I think I had.

Chapter Twenty-Four

After the war was over, life seemed to get back on track. With rationing no longer required, people could buy anything they wanted so long as it was available and they had the money. New automobiles weren't on the market immediately as the automobile plants had to be re-configured from war manufacturing to domestic production. But soon I began to see new cars on the street, and they could be seen in showrooms, too.

People had gotten so used to the war that it was a bit of jolt to return to life as it had been before. But it very quickly became evident that there would be no going back. At first there were few soldiers or sailors, but within a few months when they began to be demobilized, they were everywhere. I read in the newspaper that many of them were returning to college and as a result college enrollments were booming.

Entertainment began to change, too. I rarely went to movies, so I didn't know much of what was popular. Earlier people had talked about Mary Pickford and Douglas Fairbanks, and I didn't really know about them. I had heard of Charlie Chaplin, but even then it wasn't because I had seen him in films. I had only heard people talk about his Little Tramp. For some reason they seemed to love him; maybe he spoke to them in some language without words for the movies were silent until the late 20s. Then they began to talk about Elizabeth Taylor and Mickey Rooney and others who had no attraction for me. For some reason people regarded movie stars as glamorous, maybe because so much of the movies was about people who lived exotic lives different from their everyday lives.

Later on, radio and television added their flavor to American life, but they weren't for me. I heard programs like "Lum 'n Abner" and "Fibber McGee and Mollie," but they didn't have any attraction for me. "Amos and Andy" I thought was silly. If I had the chance to listen to radio, I wanted to listen to Miss Aimee; she was the one who spoke to me.

Then after Miss Aimee was gone, television began to replace radio. Sometimes in the evening, I walked past department stores or hardware stores where televisions were playing and people were standing on the sidewalks watching. I didn't understand the attraction. It was all just lines and dots to me; snow at first, people called it. Then later, color television was invented, and that didn't attract me either. There was something missing from all of this that I needed and which movies, radio, and television simply did not provide.

Actually I thought my life was quite satisfying. The children at the care center needed me, and I needed them. I didn't think I should need anything else. After Jeannie ran off with a traveling salesman, Mrs. Watson took in a homeless girl named Martha who began to fill in for Jeannie. She wasn't as attentive to her duties as Jeannie had been, but Mrs. Watson saw she had a need and thought maybe it could be satisfied by her working at the boarding house.

"You see, Alex, she just hasn't had any upbringing. All she needs is a little training."

The times I watched Martha or helped out I thought she needed more than a little training. But Mrs. Watson felt she was doing some good just by giving her a place to stay, and I didn't want to interfere. Still I noticed that when she was away from Mrs. Watson she behaved differently. She liked to sit in the living room with the men and talk with them as they listened to the radio or played cards or checkers. Maybe it was innocent, but with my upbringing from the Sisters of Mercy I was skeptical.

Jeannie sent Mrs. Watson and me one postcard. It came from Olathe, Kansas where she was living with her husband; she told us they had gotten married. It was a jokey card with a creature called a "jack a lope" on it, a combination jackrabbit and antelope. All she wrote was, "We're settled down here and have our own place. Wish you could see it. Bob (her husband) is doing well, and we're planning a honeymoon trip. Love, Jeannie."

As I thought about what living in Olathe, Kansas must be like, I also began to wonder about the attraction of travel. Maybe there was something to wanting to see other places; maybe Jeannie had been right. I didn't seem to have the urge, however. I did have one desire, though: I wanted to see snow. Living in southern California, I never had experienced it. Of course, I knew about it, but reading of snow or hearing people talk isn't the same as walking in it or feeling the flakes on one's face as they drift down. I had seen the whites of mountain tops which people said was snow, but even that wasn't enough. I had to walk in it myself, to feel the cold, to absorb the freshness of a brisk wind carrying snow along the ground.

On a day in January I went to the bus depot to go where there was snow. "I want to buy a ticket."

"Where to?"

"Where there is snow."

He studied me. "Oregon? Washington? Some other state?"

"No. I understand there is snow in California."

"Well, that's so. There is. Why don't you just go up the mountain?

"Does the bus go up there?"

"Almost. It'll take you to where you can walk to it."

"How much?"

He told me, I paid, and received a ticket.

I reported to the bus station on a Sunday afternoon to go see snow. I took along a winter coat and gloves which I hardly ever wore in southern California.

When the bus reached my destination, I got out and walked around. There was a very small building which served as a combination gasoline station and bus stop. I walked a few hundred yards away from it, up a slight rise to where there was snow on the ground. I suppose I have to admit to myself that it was a letdown. Somehow I had expected snow to be something more than just white and cold and somewhat unpleasant. Even in my coat and gloves, I felt chilled.

But since I was there I bent down and picked up some of it, fashioning a snowball and then throwing it. Maybe if I had had someone with me, the experience would have been better. As it was, however, I very quickly decided that I did not like snow, and I wanted to get back as soon as possible. I walked back to the bus stop and waited inside for the return trip.

Objectively, I imagine I have to admit that my life was quite circumscribed, even boring. I liked working with the children, I enjoyed reading, and there didn't seem to be much else to my life. The adventures I experienced as I read were so grand and even spectacular that I never thought I could ever realize anything comparable in my everyday life. But then everyday life wasn't for that sort of thing. That's what books were for. In fact, I probably would have protested if someone had tried to meld the two.

One Sunday afternoon I was sitting in my room reading, when the electricity went off and the world simply stopped. Everything ended. There was no sound: no television, no radio, no clock ticking, nothing audible. Such noise as people surround themselves with perhaps is a type of aural comfort of faith, and when it's removed, they revert to some primitive state of silence. They're left alone to fend for ourselves. How strange to have true silence in this world of overpowering noise. Was the world meant to be like this with my ear drums vibrating continuously to the endless reverberation of sound? It is what is. Only when it all stops can we hear the silence. It's like trying to see the stars from a lighted city—they're there but we can't see them. We've blinded ourselves. And I suppose we have also deafened ourselves. In a way it was disappointing when the electricity came back on again, even though I could read better by the light of a light bulb than by mere daylight.

Did I ever admit to myself during those years that I was getting older, that I was becoming a mature woman? I don't remember that I ever stopped to think about it, but there I was passing thirty, becoming middle-aged, and hardly aware of it. I remember a radio soap opera called "The Romance of Helen Trent" in which the question was asked, "Can love come to a woman after thirty-five?" I never felt the need for romance in my life. I suppose Jeannie in Olathe, Kansas needed it, but such was not my desire. To be truthful I went along from day to day, not examining, but not finding fault either. Life was predictable and regular. Why should I want to change it?

Chapter Twenty-Five

I have learned in my more than eighty-nine years that life creeps up on us at times, giving no advance notice, no warning, and suddenly, something occurs for which we have had subtle foreshadowing, but which we ignored. Why are we like this? Why am I like this? I don't fully understand, but I know that these surprises are difficult to deal with. Oh, yes, I should have been paying closer attention, but who among us actually does?

One of these bombshells exploded when Mrs. Watson told me she was closing her boarding house, going out of business, selling the house, and retiring. I had seen the signs, of course: a dwindling number of residents, less and less call for what she offered—a homey atmosphere which promised and delivered family values. There simply was no longer any market for the goods she was selling. She was down to two faithful residents beyond me, but they were aging also, just as she had, and as she saw it, it was time for her to accept time's depredations.

Were we truly mature and adult, we would accept all of this as a matter of course, plodding wearily onward with banner held high. We aren't.

By itself this was enough to destroy my sense of comfort, to uproot me, to re-define my world in terms that weren't immediately pleasant nor that I was eager to accept. However, on we must go.

The money provided me by the U. S. Navy following Edward's death had accrued sufficient interest that I could afford to buy my own house with some left over. I found a two-bedroom "cottage," as it was called, which appealed to me. I suppose what really attracted me was both the front and back yards, rife with blooms and bursting with nature's bounty. There were a few trees also, so that I could feel I was in my own slight way connected with nature.

About the same time as Mrs. Watson's closing up her boarding house and shunting all of us residents out into the maelstrom of American society, I learned that the Sisters of Mercy Orphanage was being discontinued. There had been less and less call for orphanages over the years, and it appeared that the institution had outlived its social function. The sisters had aged beyond what was useful or effective for serving the orphans, the building had deteriorated, and the bishop decreed that the orphanage was to be no more.

For some inexplicable reason the closing of the orphanage affected me deeply. I had entertained no affection for the home or for the sisters—in fact, I had maintained no contact with any of my fellow residents since leaving—yet I found myself teary-eyed and nostalgic for it. But as I thought about it, I saw that perhaps what I was truly feeling pain for was my former self; so long as the institution continued, so, too, did I in my earlier manifestation. Now, with it gone, I had to accept myself as an aging widow—actually not really a widow, legally—who had few ties to anyone or anything in society.

On a whim I walked past the orphanage one day, to try to satisfy myself that it truly was of the past. Where the building had stood was a vacant lot with signs proclaiming it as the site of a future development—a building of offices for insurance salesman, health officials, and other such twentieth century occupations. Despite my hard-headed objectivity or pragmatism, I felt some sense of grief, a quickening of the soul seeking to reaffirm my earlier self. Were the meager tears I shed tears of selfishness? I didn't truly know. All I could see was that it had been effaced from the earth, taking with it all of my previous life, all of my youth, and all that I had known and experienced. Like a monument gradually reduced in size by wind and rain, so, too, were my memories being reduced; in a process which seemed to mock the one whereby we grew up and matured, aged, and realized some sort of fruition, this reverse process was taking away the past and leaving nothing in its place except hazy memories. They became less defined every day and were harder and harder to bring to the surface of my mind. Only in my dreams at night did the orphanage still exist. There, the sisters still bossed everyone around with the authority of natural tyrants, the children stood up under their trials with equanimity, and I forged on into the unknowing and uncaring future.

This growing older I realized was a bigger trial than I had ever anticipated. What preparation had I been given which would allow me to deal with all of this apparently meaningless and undeniable change? I didn't want any of it, but I was powerless in the face of some greater authority than I, some indefinable force which held me in its rough, chapped hands and worked its will with me as it does with everyone. Tears were meaningless in the face of such impersonal and uncaring force. All I could do was plod wearily onward, hoping against hope that it wouldn't turn out negatively.

Chapter Twenty-Six

I have fought with being a woman all my life. There was a time when I did not wish to be a woman; this was when I was at the Sisters of Mercy. But later on I guess I accepted my role as one of God's downtrodden ones. In the early part of the twentieth century, women had very few privileges, and they certainly were not accorded equal rights. The passage of the 19th amendment to the Constitution in 1920 did redress some of the imbalance, but it seemed to me all it did was make women equally to blame for whatever was wrong with society. Who wanted that? Not I.

As I approached my teens, I recognized that the older girls shared some secret which bound them together and which excluded the rest of us. I didn't have any idea what it was and I was curious, but I think it didn't bother me. I often caught them whispering to each other and even giggling which behavior I didn't wish to engage in at all.

Then one day I started to bleed. What was happening I had no idea. When I reported to Sister Armenia, our nurse, she didn't seem to take my sickness to heart. "Oh, so now you've started," is all she said at first.

"But Sister, something is wrong with me. I'm bleeding."

"Yes, child, I know, but there is nothing wrong. This is what you will have to go through every month from now on. It means you are a woman."

At thirteen I did not wish to be a woman. However, I had recognized the swelling of my breasts so that they could no longer be ignored. I had tried to pretend that nothing was happening, but obviously something was. The added body hair was simply an embarrassment, and I began to act like some of the other girls, shying away from letting anyone see me naked. This wasn't challenging as the sisters discouraged anybody from showing her body unnecessarily. Now, I had to face it.

With Sister Armenia's instruction and encouragement, I taught myself how to deal with this new problem. I never saw any evidence that the sisters at the home had to deal with this, but I suppose they did. Apparently they refused to admit that they were human. From their habits one would never have guessed that they had breasts at all.

Over the years I dealt with being a woman as many women before and since have; it was simply a part of my equation. Truthfully, however, I never regretted it when my periods stopped. I never missed them. What good had they done me? I would never have children of my own. They were just a monthly trial that had to be accepted. Other women called them the curse, the monthlies, or the rag.

When they first started, Sister Armenia had told me this was God's way of making me a woman. They were a bother, of course, as in those days no one talked of such matters, and there were no products sold to deal with such womanly matters. I learned to deal with them the same as the older girls did. They used discarded or worn-out clothing cut into strips for rags. Then afterwards, the rags were washed out and dried and put way to be used again the next month.

When they stopped, I thought there might be something wrong. But other women told me it was a blessing, and I saw it was as if a curse had been lifted. Now I no longer had to deal with the mess of my body every month. It was a great relief. Maybe I had come full circle—from an innocent girl to an old woman who no longer was faced with this monthly trial.

It seems to me that I am less mercurial in my feelings today, also. When I was a younger woman, I often experienced weird and unexplainable feelings. These could be on nearly anything, and they were often quite intense feelings of hate, affection or love, jealousy, or extreme rage. They were so strong that I felt people must see them in my face and often I turned away to try to hide my inner core.

At first I didn't understand this at all, wondering what was happening to me, at times wondering if I was losing my mind. Only after some time did I begin to recognize these feelings as leading up to my periods.

Later on I found that there was a term for this: PMS, or Pre-Menstrual Syndrome. Of course, other women knew what I was going through, and they tended to be quite sympathetic. Men certainly did not, but then I had grown used to men putting me down anyway—"Just a woman" and so on—so I never expected a man to understand.

All in all, I have to say that this life—or the life I have lived—hasn't been easy. Of course, there have been satisfactions, but there were times when I regretted the short span Edward and I enjoyed. It had been perfect or so nearly so that I couldn't have improved on it. Yet even granting that it would be impossible to repeat, I wanted it again. Not with anyone else, of course; I couldn't hope to enjoy with any man what I had shared with Edward.

I had heard women talk of making love—with reverence, it seemed—but I didn't really understand what the phrase meant. Making love I knew was equated with sex, but sex I wanted nothing to do with. Sex was what men were after, it was what the sisters cautioned us against, and it was what was embarrassing to me. I was taught to be ashamed of my sex, both as a woman and as an embodiment of sexual urges or parts. Making love meant a man and a woman doing it together, and this was wrong except in marriage. I suppose there was a residue of guilt in me about what I had enjoyed with Edward.

But later, after I thought about it, I saw that making love could be literal. For if a man and a woman truly loved each other, and they did truly make love, the product could be a baby, and what was a baby, but love embodied? Maybe this was what God intended with sex, that a man and a woman should make love, should create a baby which is the best of all living creations and which means love. Making love for me became a way of thinking about making babies, and after that it became something not dirty or shameful but something to revel in, something to be proud of, something to glorify God by. I think this allowed me to come to acceptance of what Edward and I had shared—not as something dirty or something to be ashamed of but as something to be proud of. I had been loved, and I had loved in return.

As a result I felt sorry for the lonely, alone women, with their sterile, empty lives. Lives without family, without true friends, even without men—after all, who needed men?—how could they go on with only God in their lives? Surely He wasn't enough. It wouldn't be enough for me. I promised that I would never live as a sister of Mercy. I would keep the love Edward and I had shared. Nor did I need a ring. If I wore a ring on my ring finger, it wouldn't be symbolic—it would be an actual ring for a real marriage—not some fake of a promise to some ethereal creature that might not even exist. If I had to I'd buy my own ring, but it wouldn't be a wedding to God; that I knew.

Chapter Twenty-Seven

Sin is a word I have known all my life, but I think I don't actually know what it means. Oh, I know what the sisters of Mercy wanted us to confess. They talked about sin quite regularly, and told us we had to confess all of our sins. In our catechism classes we learned the difference between mortal and venial sins, why I don't know, for I don't believe there was a single mortal sin in the whole school. Maybe the sisters had to confess mortal sins, but I'm sure the priest must have tired of hearing us confess our trivial offenses: "I envied the grades of my classmate, I was angry, I didn't do my daily chores with the proper attitude, I forget to say my prayers." What is truly sinful about any of those? Surely true sin deserves much more than consideration of such trivia.

We learned about original sin; that was the one we were born with and over which we had no control. How could we be held responsible for it then if we had nothing to do with it? Yes, sin can be an act of commission or an act of omission, but original sin which came from Adam? Where is the sense in that? We didn't even know from Adam except that he and Eve were guilty of disobeying God.

We were told that sin was a deliberate violation of the will of God attributable to human pride, self-centeredness, and disobedience. It is in essence human nature in rebellion against God. Where this became most challenging to me was in the notion that "thinking" about doing something was as much a sin as actually "doing" something. So if I thought about stealing somebody else's apple, for example, I was guilty of actually stealing it.

This concept strains my brain. How can thinking about anything be equated with actually doing the act? Right from the start, then, I didn't understand what the sisters meant when they tried to teach us about sins and sinning. Some theologian must have dreamed up this concept in order to make Roman Catholics feel guilt. For guilt was rampant among my fellow orphans, and guilt was common commerce among the sisters. Guilt was available for any sister to impose onto any six-year-old who refused to finish her oatmeal at breakfast, or any thirteen-year-old who handed in a paper which wasn't done quite neatly enough. But in looking back, I realize just how effective guilt was at controlling us. In fact the residue of the sisters' teaching stays with me yet today, for I can feel guilty over nearly anything. I think I read somewhere that guilt is the gift that keeps on giving, and this I know to be true. For guilt I have the sisters to thank.

The distinction between mortal sins and venial sins seemed easier to understand. A mortal sin is a deliberate turning away from God, done willingly and knowingly, and it cuts the sinner off from God's grace. Claudius in *Hamlet* is guilty of a mortal sin, and he knows it; that's why he can't be optimistic about his prayers going up to heaven since he is unwilling to give up what he has gained by killing his brother.

A venial sin is less important and is committed with less self-awareness of wrongdoing. Since it isn't a deliberate turning away from God, it doesn't block the flow of sanctifying grace. Maybe the sisters were guilty of mortal sins; perhaps some of them actually hated their routine, or maybe they engaged in secret practices we didn't know about. But school girls? I simply couldn't swallow the concept. Our lives were trivial, made up of niggling details, and our sins, too, were trivial and inconsequential. Perhaps, I'm thinking today, it was a sin of the sisters to imbue us with this load of guilt which I and I'll warrant many of my classmates carry on our rounded shoulders yet today. Maybe that was a sin.

One difference I note between what I was taught at the Sisters of Mercy orphanage and their theology compared to the church I attend today is that people at the church I attend now do not focus on sin. They focus on doing good deeds, on helping others. Call this humanism if you like, the distinction doesn't seem to matter to me, but I believe the parishioners are not burdened with such a load of guilt. For in truth, how does guilt aid anyone? How does guilt help us to get through our daily lives? Because we feel guilty, we help others? This is a difficult concept for me.

However, I read somewhere that one of the Devil's greatest wiles is to persuade us that he doesn't exist. Is that what I'm about here? If I don't believe in sin, am I denying the Devil's existence and by extension Christ's and God's existence? Again I suppose I'd have to consult a theologian to try to resolve this as I don't seem capable of doing it myself.

Still, I have tried to forget about sin and guilt. Yes, I certainly know right from wrong, and I do consistently try to do the right things, but where the wrong things—such as speaking shortly or harshly to someone—become sin is where I am lost at sea with no sextant. The whole concept appears to be a trivialization of a much more weighty matter. For a thinking person this is a challenging and probably irresolvable matter.

Chapter Twenty-Eight

I was astounded one night to wake and find myself crying. In my dream I had been suffering some great trauma the outline of which was all that was available to me. Yet, when I awoke, both of my eyes were wet with tears. What sort of connection was there between my dreams and my physical self that permitted my eyes to actually cry while I was asleep? I think there had been children in the dream and some threat to them, but beyond that, I couldn't remember. What amazed me, however, was the tears.

What extra-sensory connection existed between the dreams in my brain and my tear ducts? Surely there was something going on here which escaped me entirely. Tears had never come easily to me, even when I was a girl. When I fell or was hurt in some way, I dealt with it. If I had to be punished, then I took the punishment and tried not to react, especially with tears. Tears were weakness, I suppose I felt, so I never cried.

All my life I have had to hide my feelings. Oh, not at first. At first I didn't know the sisters punished feelings. I didn't realize that they— who evinced no feelings—resented them in others, even children. So I was punished for crying, for laughing, even for smiling. What sort of person punishes children for being alive? But maybe it was because they envied the children—since they weren't alive maybe they resented the children's enjoyment of life.

It is possible that one or two of the sisters also doubted. Their reward was to be heaven, the afterlife. But what if this were all a lie? What then? They would feel cheated, never having felt love, or hate, or envy or anything—no emotion. All for a false premise. Of course later on I saw that to display emotion meant trusting others. But I didn't know that at first. At first I was like the sisters: an automaton. They taught me well.

As I had matured I had come to regard sleep as a release or a deliverance from life. In my dreams I was young again, and everything seemed to float along in an ethereal way with no threat of any kind. Thus, I looked forward to going to bed every night. When sleep came, the dreams came, too, and they were comforting and warm. At times when I woke in the morning, I was disappointed that I couldn't continue to sleep and dream. Sleep and dreaming became a retreat from life. Was this a form of death wish? All I know is that the dreams were wonderfully reassuring.

Thus, when I woke crying, I was upset that my world had turned. Was this some sort of existential release of my soul that allowed me to cry while I was asleep and had gladly relinquished control? I suppose I could have been angry at my body for betraying me this way, but I wasn't. Instead I felt something close to awe: recognition that my body exhibited behavior over which I had no control and which might actually be better for me. Truthfully, I didn't understand it.

I wiped my tears away and went back to sleep.

Chapter Twenty-Nine

I have combated religion all along this strenuous life path I have pursued. I can't say that I either won or lost; mostly it has been a type of stand-off. In truth, the Sisters of Mercy left me with such a bad taste in my mouth that when I left the orphanage I didn't care if I never saw the inside of a church again. But their methods proved appallingly effective, for the very next Sunday, there I was, kneeling in the pew at St. Agnes' Catholic Church, following along and beating my breast at the proper time.

Mostly this was because it was what I knew and was comfortable with. Perhaps comfortable is the wrong word; at any rate it is what I had experienced and what I could assume over my existence like a winter coat that covers up everything underneath. But even though it was covered up, there were some doubts peeking out, asking to see the light of reason. Why was the Roman Catholic religion as the sisters instilled it into us so authoritarian? Surely in God's kingdom there ought to be room for a modicum of skepticism if not doubt. But no, no question—no matter how innocent—was brooked by the good sisters. Doubt was the tool of the devil, and those who doubted were consigned to perdition.

What was missing from the sisters' approach to religion was any thinking. In fact, any of us who evinced thinking in our approach to religion were punished. Thus, we learned to shove any doubt back down into our cores where, unfortunately, like kneaded bread dough, it continued to expand and seek escape. It was bound to come out.

Only after I left the orphanage and came across a book which mentioned Margery Kempe did I come to see that perhaps religion didn't have to be institutionalized, that a person could choose for herself what direction to take and how to serve God.

When I read about Margery Kempe, I began to find myself. She renounced the world, her husband, her children, and set out to glorify God. Where had her conviction come from? I wanted to be like her, but I was filled with doubt. I doubted the church, the sisters, myself—at times I even doubted God. How could I ever be like Margery Kempe? How had she ever found the courage to dispute her husband and all of society, for in those days of the 14th and 15th century women were even lesser creatures than in the 20th century. Yet she had and, despite being unable to read or write, she triumphed.

In her meeting with the Archbishop of Canterbury, she was received respectfully, and later she successfully defended herself against charges of heresy and being a Lollard before the Archbishop of York. And all of this was after giving birth to fourteen children and making her husband agree to foreswear having sex with her.

What all of this seemed to be saying to me was that religion was too important to be left to the clerics.

Then as I was reading in an anthology of American Literature I came across the poetry of Emily Dickinson who said she worshiped in the great outdoors, in the great cathedral of the sky. Was this the path I should follow?

I knew that organized religion had caused great harm among people it was supposed to be assisting along the road to salvation. The intolerance of the Catholic Church was an ugly smear of hatred across the pages of the history of the church.

Then I happened to pick up a book, *Pigeon Feathers*, by John Updike. In the title story, I read about David handling the pigeons; I saw "He was robed in this certainty: that the God who had lavished such craft upon these worthless birds would not destroy His whole Creation by refusing to let David live forever." Wasn't this truly affirmative of God's benevolence? Surely in this kingdom there was a place for me.

Gradually I came to terms with my doubts and began to celebrate the mysteries of spiritualism. Usually it was in church, but not always. Sometimes I just walked outdoors and studied trees, leaves, grass, and birds. For there was no doubt in my mind that God must reside in living creatures. And if he reposed in a robin or a sparrow, a blade of grass or a dandelion, why not in me?

I think by now I have come to some peace with my God. He is in everything, and He is in me. If this be heresy, then I, too, ought to be tried. I suppose I will be found wanting, but like Margery Kempe, I intend to follow my own path.

Chapter Thirty

It just doesn't seem right that I should be eighty-nine years old. How did this ever happen, anyway? I lived a good life, tried to live as a person should, emulating Christ, and here I am having to accept that I'm actually eighty-nine years old. And what about next year? Then I'll be ninety. And the year after, I'll enter my tenth decade of life. This just doesn't seem possible.

Oh, I've lived and done things. I've enjoyed the love of a man, I've shared love with women and children—children, especially—but when I look into the mirror I do not recognize the image that appears there. Is it maybe some creature suffering at the hands of the witch in "Snow White"? Her hair has almost no color left, and it flies all over as if each strand were a teenager searching for his or her own way into a concert. And the lines. Who ever knew at age twenty-two, for example, that the face would become such a repository of life actions with lines intersecting and bisecting so that they're almost impossible to make sense of? Too many lines for me. But there they are.

Some of the lines are good. The creases at the corners of my eyes reveal smiles, smiles of the years that helped to keep my spirits up and may have helped brighten other people's days, too. Those lines say that I have lived and that I have enjoyed what happened to me. But there are other, less positive ones. There are cracks and blemishes which require makeup to hide. But who, at my age, wears makeup? Not I.

I've seen other women as old as I am—some even younger—who fight against the depredations of time by smearing on the rouge and face powder and topping it off with a garish shade of lipstick. Surely this is what Hamlet was talking about in act five when he protested about women wearing make-up. This is what we come to. I refuse.

Somehow it seems unfair that I am eighty-nine. Of course, I don't know what alternative there is. Fortunately I didn't die along the way, so I suppose I do need to give thanks. But who can be thankful for a tired old body that no longer performs? As the comedian says, everything hurts and what doesn't hurt doesn't work. Aches and pains in the morning are only the beginning. Stumble against a table or a chair and carry the bruise for a week afterwards. And those bruises—these aren't grade school or high school bruises; these are Olympic-sized bruises of multi-colored hues: reds, oranges, pinks, and purples which as a teenager we might have bragged about, but today, they're objects of shame. I suppose it's a good thing I don't live with anyone else as those bruises might cause him (or her) to be accused of abuse. No, the bruises are mine and mine only, caused primarily by carelessness.

Falling is something else. I've fallen, and when a person gets on in years as I am, falls are serious. Old people should wear pillows on all parts of their anatomy, even their elbows. When I shattered my right elbow five years ago, that was hellish. Not only could I not use that arm, but I had to eat with my left hand. Of course, I couldn't be allowed to live on my own, so I had to be shunted into one of those institutions where dying is treated as a natural and inevitable part of life. Not for me. Despite my elbow which sported its cast, I wasn't about to die.

When the therapist came to check up on me and asked if I ever exercised, I proudly answered, "I exercise every day." I had counted the steps around the quad on the floor where I resided; it was one hundred and sixty steps. Assuming that my steps were one yard each, I figured out that if I did eleven laps, that equaled 1,760 yards or one mile. So I walked eleven laps every night.

The therapist refused to believe me. Here I was, eighty-four years old, telling the truth, and this twenty-something junior doctor patently refused to believe me. So I had to demonstrate. Then she had to accept me, despite harboring her own doubts.

I could tell while I was sequestered in that place that no one was expected ever to leave. But my primary motivation in getting well was that I return home and resume my independence. In fact, I suspect they were surprised that I ever got the cast removed from my elbow and could use my arm again.

When I left, they gave me a party. Maybe nobody had ever gone home from this place before. Well, I did.

But the challenging and daunting part of my life was that I had more of such experiences to look forward to. I didn't want to fall again, but as sure as I'm eighty-nine going on ninety, I will fall again. What will it be next time? A hip? An arm? Maybe a leg? Who knows how long it will take for the body to heal? Maybe I won't be coming home next time. From the perspective of almost nine complete decades, life doesn't hold out much promise.

Who knew when we were grade schoolers or high schoolers that any of us would ever get to be this age? When I was in grade school, anyone over twenty-one was old, and people over thirty were ancient. I don't think I ever even differentiated between say thirty and sixty; people were simply old. But as I've gotten older, I've realized that age is entirely relative. I saw in the newspaper a report of a study that reflected how people regard age. People aged sixty said anyone over seventy is old. People who were seventy said that eighty was old. And anyone who was eighty said it was ninety. No one wants to be old. I smile when I remember that joke of the man who was celebrating his eightieth birthday and asked what his birthday wish was. "Oh, to be seventy again," he said. And despite seeing the humor in the statement, I see what he meant. I wouldn't mind being seventy again, having seen what eighty-nine looks like.

Still I say my daily prayers and give thanks to God. I envy nature's rebirth each spring, and I enjoy the bountiful harvest every year, not knowing whether this will be my last one. But I think I'm ready. God's kingdom is unending and limitless, and if it has room for someone of my age and character, then I have to prepare myself. God's will be done.